STO

FRIEN
OF ACPL
P9-CCU-859

Children of the U. S. A.

Stories from the South

A STORY FROM EACH OF THE SOUTHERN STATES
AND FROM OUR LANDS IN THE CARIBBEAN

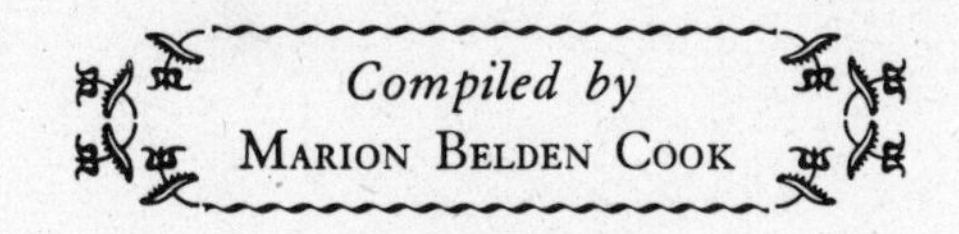

Illustrated by MILLARD MCGEE

SILVER BURDETT COMPANY

NEW YORK CHICAGO SAN FRANCISCO

PRINTED IN THE UNITED STATES OF AMERICA

Stories in this Book

Stories from the Territories

To the Boys and Girls Who Read This Book:

All the stories in the three books, CHILDREN OF THE U. S. A., were written to tell you how boys and girls live and work and play in each of the states and principal territories of the United States of America.

STORIES FROM THE EAST AND NORTH is about boys and girls who live in the northern states, east of the Mississippi River. On the map in the front of the book you will find these states. This book also includes a story from the District of Columbia.

STORIES FROM THE SOUTH is about boys and girls in the southern states, both east and west of the Mississippi River. In this book there are also stories from our lands in the Caribbean Sea: the Panama Canal Zone, Puerto Rico, and the Virgin Islands. Again you will find maps showing the states and the territories where the stories take place.

STORIES FROM THE WEST is about boys and girls in the remaining states, between the Mississippi River and the Pacific Ocean. This book also includes stories from the territories of the Pacific: Alaska, the Hawaiian Islands, Guam, and the Philippines. Although the Philippine Islands will soon be an independent republic, they have been included among the stories from the territories because of their long and close association with the United States of America. In this book, as in the other two books, you will find maps showing where the stories take place.

To become acquainted with boys and girls from each state and from each of the principal territories, you will want to read the three books, CHILDREN OF THE U. S. A.

MARION BELDEN COOK

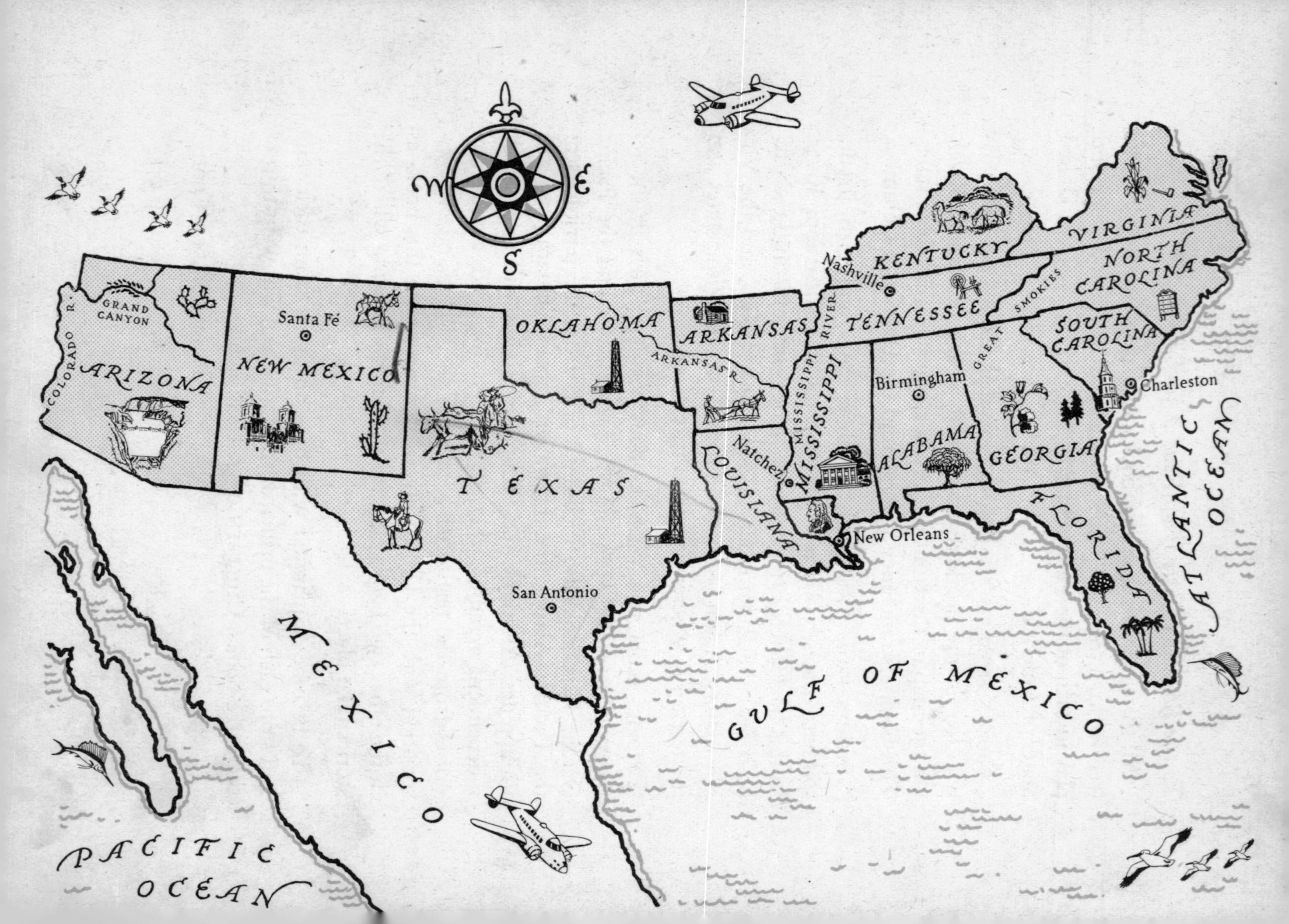

W
E
S
COLORADO R.
GRAND CANYON
ARIZONA
Santa Fé
NEW MEXICO
OKLAHOMA
ARKANSAS R.
TEXAS
San Antonio
ARKANSAS
LOUISIANA
Natchez
MISSISSIPPI RIVER
MISSISSIPPI
New Orleans
Nashville
KENTUCKY
TENNESSEE
VIRGINIA
NORTH CAROLINA
GREAT SMOKIES
SOUTH CAROLINA
Charleston
Birmingham
ALABAMA
GEORGIA
FLORIDA
ATLANTIC OCEAN
GULF OF MEXICO
MEXICO
PACIFIC OCEAN

Plantation Gold

VIRGINIA

ON a Friday afternoon in early January, a school bus rolled past woodland and fields and large and small farmhouses in southern Virginia. The bus rattled across a bridge, climbed a long hill, and stopped on the ridge top to let out six children. Emmett and Jane More, whose father was a tenant farmer, lived in the neat little house close to the highway. The four young Allens belonged to "Long Ridge," the big square white house half a mile away on the broad top of the ridge.

As they started down the plantation road toward "Long Ridge," Dick Allen stopped on the roadside.

"Let's see—" he said, "I want to know what they've done today. Oh, I can smell it. Wood smoke. They're burning a tobacco plant bed. Father said they would if the wind didn't rise. Let's go by there."

"Can't." His sister Mary was sorry. "Got to get home to feed my chickens."

"We'll go!" "We'll go!" shouted Lewis and Susie, the younger Allens, running back up the road.

Mr. Allen and his three tenant farmers had almost finished the burning. They were rounding up the half-burnt logs. Dick threw on armfuls of brush, to make the smoldering logs blaze. On this plot, made fine and fertile and free from weed seeds by burning, the tiny precious tobacco seed would be planted.

"Well, it's feeding time," Mr. Allen said presently to his helpers. "Jim, go by the pasture and bring the cows. Henry, I'll get out the corn by the time you give the horses their hay. Abe, you can finish rounding up this fire. Come, Susie, you and Lewis. Let's go home."

Dick fell into step beside his father. "I've decided about my this year's crop, Father. Tobacco."

"Oh! You think you want tobacco, do you?" Mr. Allen said slowly.

"Yes, Father."

On "Long Ridge," as on most farms in the community, the children had crops and stock of their own. They began with garden patches and a few chickens or ducks.

Later, they had crop plants, cattle, and hogs. All the Allen children belonged to the 4–H Club, the splendid organization that encourages and directs children's farm work.

"Why not another corn crop, Dick? or cotton?" Mr. Allen asked after a brief silence.

"Why not tobacco, Father?"

"We-ell, cotton and corn are good fellows who don't call on you for winter work, and they give you a summer vacation. Tobacco is a spoiled gentleman. You must come when he calls, and you must wait on him thirteen months in the year."

Susie laughed. "What a funny thing to say!—with just twelve months in a year."

"Figure it out for yourself, Miss Susie," replied her father. "Last year in January we burned a plant bed for tobacco. We sowed the seed, transplanted the plants to the field, tended the crop, cured it in the barn, and put it in the packhouse. Now it is January again. This week we've been ordering and sorting tobacco, to take to market next week. Isn't that a thirteen-month crop?"

"It certainly is!" Susie agreed emphatically.

"I know tobacco takes a lot of work," said Dick, "but it's our best-paying money crop. I want something I'm sure will bring enough to buy a bicycle."

"Ah, son, there is nothing sure about any farm crop. The only sure thing, especially about tobacco, is the work."

"I'm not afraid of work," declared Dick.

"All right," agreed his father. "If you want a tobacco crop, you may have it. I'll even give you a special advantage—a little packet of seed, Plantation Gold, a new variety of our Orinoko tobacco."

"Plantation Gold and Orinoko! Why two names?" asked Lewis.

"They are like your two names, Lewis and Allen. Plantation Gold is the name of this special kind, and Orinoko is the family, or type, name. The English, who came to Virginia in 1607, found the Indians growing Orinoko, 'bright tobacco.' It has been an important crop in Virginia ever since."

Dick set to work with a will. He helped prepare the plant bed, raking into the fine soil the top layer of wood ashes and the fertilizer scattered by Abram More. The tobacco seed were carefully sowed by Mr. Allen's expert hand. In one corner, penned off by poles, were put the precious seed of Plantation Gold.

"What a stingy little packet of seed!" exclaimed Dick. "Not enough for a crop; just a patch."

"If these seed were plentiful, they'd not be so precious," his father reminded him. "Anyway, a small crop is best for your first try-out of tobacco. Remember, other things claim time—your school and home work. Now let's select the land for your crop."

After careful consideration, the place was chosen, a level fertile field near the highway.

During the next few weeks, the work of preparing for the tobacco crop was sandwiched between Dick's other duties. With what pride and pleasure he plowed, harrowed, fertilized his field, laid off rows, marked off hills.

Now it was May,—time to take up the tobacco plants from the bed and set them in the field. The weather was warm, but, alas! it was distressingly dry. Morning after morning the sky was blue and cloudless. Sometimes in the afternoon promising clouds billowed up—only to roll away, without giving a drop of water to the parched earth.

One such week passed, then another and another. Tobacco plants were drooping in the plant bed when they ought to be growing in the field.

Coming from school one Wednesday afternoon, Dick saw the farm men at the plant bed to which they had just hauled barrels of water. Dick joined them, to water his Plantation Gold.

"Father," he asked, "what about watering and planting our crop?"

"Not if we can help it—too much work, and bad start for the crop. We'll wait a while longer, son, hoping for rain."

"There was a good rain sign last night," said Abram More, "a ring around the moon and three stars inside the ring. That promises rain in three days—rain by Saturday."

"That's the one day I don't want rain," declared Dick. "I've got to go to 'Oak Hill' Saturday. If the bus stops running, I'll start to walk; and if my feet give out, I'll crawl on my hands and knees."

For weeks he and his friends had been looking forward to this picnic at "Oak Hill," the home of a schoolmate. It was to be more than a picnic; it was to be a great event. Their schoolmate's uncle, Dan Elwood, a famous flyer, was to be at "Oak Hill" that day.

Think of seeing Dan Elwood with your own eyes! of hearing him talk! of having him sign his name on a card that you would keep all your life! No wonder Dick was willing to have the disastrous drought last another day or two, to give him a clear free Saturday.

But Abram More's rain sign came true. On Friday morning, Dick waked to find the sky clouded. As the day wore on, the clouds thickened. Late in the afternoon, it began to drizzle. Then came a steady rain. Dick heard it at bedtime. He heard it when he waked early Saturday morning. It had rained all night. This was a perfect "season" for transplanting tobacco.

Dick knew he ought to be glad. But, oh! how could he give up that "Oak Hill" trip, to stay at home and plant his crop?

"Can't I work till bus time?" he blurted out at breakfast. "And after I get back, I'd plant tobacco all night. Or I could finish planting Monday."

His father looked at him gravely. "This 'season' will not last till Monday. It is clearing now. We may have another spell of dry weather. Dick, you chose your crop. Are you going to accept its responsibilities?"

Dick gulped. "I—I— Yes, sir."

Heavy-hearted, he followed his father to the plant bed where Abram More and Jim Jackson were already at work. With careful, expert hands, the men drew the tobacco plants and laid them in orderly piles.

Dick started toward the patch of Plantation Gold.

"Wait!" called his father. "Better let me draw those precious plants—soon as I get field work started. You can carry—No! here comes Henry at last. Henry, put these plants in the hampers and carry them to the fields."

The planting squads were ready. Every possible person had been rounded up for the urgent task. Mr. Allen had hired hands, and his three tenant farmers were helped by their wives and children. Susie and Lewis had volunteered to work with Dick.

While Dick waited for his plants, the bus came up the highway—the bus taking his friends to "Oak Hill," to Dan Elwood. It stopped at the plantation road and the driver blew sharply. Dick ran to the road.

"I can't come. Got to plant my tobacco."

The bus waited while the boys protested and urged. "Aw, come on!" "Dan Elwood! You mustn't miss him." "Let the old tobacco wait."

Dick shook his head. "Can't. Wish—I could. Can't."

The lump in his throat grew bigger as he watched the bus go down the road. Then he went slowly back to the plant bed.

Mr. Allen handed Dick a basket of plants. "Start with these, son. I'll draw more by the time you need them."

"Let me carry the basket," said Susie.

"I'll drop the plants," said Lewis.

He went along the rows, dropping a plant on each hill. Dick followed with his planting peg and set out the tobacco.

What a day! Dick had helped plant tobacco, but never

before had he worked all day long at it. Stick a hole, set a plant, firm the soil around the roots; one step forward to the next hill—stick, plant, firm; and so on and on and on. Plants by tens, by hundreds. A brief rest to eat the lunch brought to the field. A minute at the end of a row to straighten his tired back, shrug his weary shoulders, wiggle his cramped fingers. Then on with the work, hill after hill, row after row. Sundown. Twilight. Almost dark.

His father was calling. "Hey, Dick! Quitting time! How about it?"

"A few more plants, Father. I'm on the last row."

"Can you see to finish?"

"Sure. This peg could work of itself in the dark."

Right place, right depth, plant in, soil firmed.

"Hooray! I've finished. I've finished." Dick forgot he was tired and ran down the road. "Come on, Father. Let's go to supper."

The supper of sizzling fried chicken, hot rolls, and strawberry shortcake tasted good to the hungry boy. After supper Mr. Allen got up stiffly from the table.

"Well, I must go back to work. I told the boys we'd finish by moonlight setting the plants we've already drawn."

"Oh, you are so tired!" exclaimed Mrs. Allen.

"Yes. But some days on a farm a man isn't worth more than a bad nickel and other days he's worth ten dollars. This is a ten-dollar day."

"I'll help." Dick lifted himself from the table.

"No. No indeed, son. Rest and go to bed. Only men are working tonight. We'll finish by midnight."

Sunday was a soft hazy day. The plants set out on Saturday did not even wilt. The roots adjusted themselves to their new home, rootlets sought food, found it, fed the little plants.

During the sunny days that followed, the tobacco grew fast. Best of all was Dick's Plantation Gold, which he cultivated and tended faithfully. Mary said teasingly that he had a name for each plant and went to the field every day to talk to his pets.

One Saturday in early August, Mr. Allen, on his way to a hay field, was halted by Dick's call.

"Hey, Father! Come by and look at my tobacco. Isn't it grand?"

"Indeed it is," Mr. Allen agreed heartily.

The beautiful plants had developed so evenly their tops were as level as a floor. The leaves were smooth and soft as satin; the upper leaves were still green, but the lower ones had a golden tinge.

"A hot day like this, you can almost see it grow and get ripe. Tobacco isn't such a hard gentleman to wait on, after all," Dick said. "He gives me time to go fishing and play ball. He even let me off a whole week last month, to go to Scout camp. And think of the A-1 bicycle he's going to give me this fall! I'll bet my Plantation Gold will top the market."

"It's the best tobacco I ever saw," said Mr. Allen. "You must save seed from it for all our next year's crop. It is ripening fast. We'll pull the bottom leaves Monday and cure them in the first barn. You've a fine crop, son, and you deserve it. You've worked like a man."

Mr. Allen turned to go, then paused.

"Dick, I reckon you'd better come and help us get in the hay. We don't want it to get wet. I don't like the look of those clouds in the west."

"Whew!" exclaimed Dick. "They're boiling up—real storm-clouds. Let me run the rake, Father."

But that job was not to be finished. The clouds massed rapidly, great tumbling dark heaps red at the edges.

"Wind," predicted Jim Jackson.

"Worse, I'm afraid," said Mr. Allen. "Jim, hurry to the stable with the team. Come, Dick. Let's run to the house."

They ran to shelter just as the storm swooped down.

There was a great rush of wind—a brief lull—a longer, harder blast with an icy edge. Mowed hay swept in great waves across the field. Tall corn flattened to the ground. The branches of the trees lashed wildly about.

For minutes that seemed hours, Dick stood beside his father at a window, not moving, not speaking.

At last Dick gasped, "Oh—my tobacco—how'll it stand this wind?"

"Not only wind," Mr. Allen said in a low voice. "Worse is coming."

Yes. Here came hail. Great pellets of ice struck the ground with such force that they bounded up, then rattled and rolled down—so many, so huge, so fast-falling that the green earth was whitened.

"Father, my tobacco will be ruined!" cried Dick.

Mr. Allen put a steadying hand on Dick's shoulder. "Son, be a man. Take it standing."

What a cruel, pitiless storm! Its path was narrow and not very long, but its full force came on "Long Ridge." In half an hour, it pelted down the crops and blasted the year's harvest hopes.

As quickly as the storm had come, it went away. The wind subsided, the hail ceased, the clouds lightened, the sun shone on the land covered with broken boughs and leaves and whitened with hail.

Dick went out, up the road, straight to his tobacco field. Surely, surely the storm must have spared that one little field. But no. It had wrecked and ruined the cherished crop. The ground was littered with broken plants and torn leaves. Every leaf left on a stalk was riddled with hail holes. Dick stood there a long time, looking at it all. Then he walked slowly back home.

The men sized up the crop situation. Some of the corn

would straighten up. Cotton was tough, and the small bolls were not much hurt. Tobacco, with big brittle leaves, had suffered most; what the wind had not broken, the hail had ruined.

"It's hard on you," Abram More turned to Dick, "being your first crop and such a fine one."

Dick tried to laugh. "Got to take bad medicine with the rest of you."

So the good folk of "Long Ridge" set to work to salvage what they could of their storm-ravaged crops. One of the jobs was to take broken tobacco leaves to the barns. In these barns, with outside big fireplaces and inside lines of fire pipes, the tobacco was to be cured, that is, thoroughly dried. Then it would be put in the packhouse. Later, the leaves would be sorted according to quality and prepared for market.

When Dick was gathering up his tobacco leaves, he had a visitor, Mr. Henderson, county farm director and leader of the 4-H Clubs.

Mr. Henderson was shocked and distressed at what the hailstorm had done to Dick's crop. "Too bad. Too bad. It was the best tobacco in our Club."

"Mr. Henderson, I was thinking," Dick began hesitantly, "such fine tobacco—Father says the best he ever saw—he wants seed for his crop next year. Mightn't other people want them? If I take good care of the plants left—to get something from my crop—" at last he blurted out his question—"could I sell some seed?"

"Dick! Smart boy!" exclaimed Mr. Henderson. "Of course, you can. I ought to have thought of that. Yes, yes. Save those seed and bring them to me. Certainly, we'll sell them."

At the proper time in the fall, Dick cut and dried the seed heads, got out the seed and took them to Mr. Henderson. Then Dick waited. At first his hopes were high, but as time went on, his spirits sank lower and lower. For in answer to his questions about sale of the seed, Mr. Henderson always said, "Not yet. Not what I wanted. Later, perhaps."

Dick stopped asking about the seed. Another failure, he thought.

Just before Christmas, the 4–H Club had a meeting, a great rally to report on the year's farm activities. The young Allens had, of course, sent in their records. Mary's chickens had done well; she had cleared nearly twenty-five dollars. Lewis and Susie had sold garden produce and some ducks; he had earned fourteen dollars and she had earned eight. Even little Susie had more than Dick. The torn green leaves of his tobacco had brought only seven dollars.

In the crowd at the hall, the Allen family separated. Mr. and Mrs. Allen followed Lewis and Susie to front seats.

Dick slipped quietly into the brightly-lighted hall and took a back seat. Mary, as silent and solemn as he, sat down beside him. They were glad when Mr. Henderson rose and called the meeting to order. One by one, he gave the records of the Club members. Only Dick's name was not mentioned. How glad he was when Mr. Henderson paused without giving that poor pitiful little record!

But Mr. Henderson had not finished. He went on, "I have saved the best for the last. It is the record of a boy who wrested victory from defeat. He worked hard and raised a magnificent tobacco crop—only to have it destroyed by a hailstorm."

Dick gasped. Was—was Mr. Henderson talking about him?

"Did this boy, then, sit down and fold his hands, sorry

for himself? Ah, no! He was too brave and too sensible for that. He had gumption enough to make that ruined crop pay by harvesting the seed to sell.

"I am happy to say I have now succeeded in selling that seed at a good price. Richard Maury Allen, please come forward and receive this check for ninety-three dollars and fifty-seven cents, in payment for the seed of your tobacco, Plantation Gold."

Mary gave Dick a shove. "Go on. Go on."

He went forward as if he were walking on air. He took the check and stood with it in his hand, dazed, while people crowded around to congratulate him. Suddenly he glanced down at the blue slip of paper and his solemn face broke into a grin.

"Father," he called, "let's go to Richmond tomorrow to get my bicycle. And I want the rest of the money in silver dollars, Christmas gifts for everybody at 'Long Ridge.' Hooray for Plantation Gold!"

The Master Carvers

AGAIN it was springtime in North Carolina. The pink bloom of the Judas trees mingled with the white blossoms of the dogwood on the grounds of Oakhurst, the home of the Thurstons in High Point. Margaret clicked open the gate in the hedge as she entered ahead of her brother, Stephen, on their way home from school.

Their mother met them at the door. "Uncle Lathrop's letter has come," she told them. "He and Annette have arrived in New York. The ship got in yesterday."

"Goody!" exclaimed Margaret. "When will Annette be here?"

"On Monday," Mrs. Thurston replied. "Uncle Lathrop will remain in New York on business for his London firm."

For months, Margaret and Stephen had anticipated the long visit of their cousin from London. Her mother, Mr. Thurston's sister, had been in England since her marriage, and the Thurstons had never seen Annette.

The following Monday evening, just as the grandfather clock struck six, there was a happy family gathering in the dining room. For dinner there was crisp fried chicken, string beans, new potatoes, carrots, spiced pear salad, and hot biscuits.

"Butter the biscuits while they're hot," Margaret told her cousin. "That's what we always say here in the South."

While Annette put butter on her first biscuit she asked, "Wasn't that a portrait of Great-Great-Great Grandfather Thurston I saw in the living room? We have one of him at home."

"Yes, my dear," replied Mrs. Thurston. "As you know, he was one of the skilled cabinet-makers of his day. He came to this country just after the Revolution."

"Mother has told me quite a bit about him," said her niece.

"Dad, why don't you tell Annette about the early cabinet-makers?" asked Stephen.

Mr. Thurston was president of a big furniture factory in High Point and was quite proud of the business he had established. Now, during dinner, he told how the well-to-do settlers of North Carolina sent over to England and France for master carvers who could make beautiful furniture and decorate the interiors of their homes.

He said, "Your great-great-great grandfather, Isaac Thurston, and the other skilled craftsmen of those early days went from home to home with their tools. They were honored guests, and their patrons consulted them about the styles of furniture. Like artists, they signed their names on the back of the pieces of furniture they made."

"Have you any furniture that Isaac Thurston made?" Annette asked.

"Yes, we have," her uncle replied. "The desk in the library and the highboy in the hall upstairs were made by him. In time," continued Mr. Thurston, "the early cabinet-makers built shops in the villages and towns and did all their work in them. Some of those shops have grown into the great factories that give our state highest rank in the production of wooden household furniture.

"The early craftsmen were familiar with the best styles of English, French, and American furniture. Some of the beautiful pieces which they made are now used as patterns by the furniture manufacturers of North Carolina. The designers go out in search of these old pieces. Copies of them have proved to be very popular."

"Stephen has done a lot of scouting around the countryside to get antiques to be copied in Dad's factory," Margaret explained to her cousin.

"It's lots of fun," Stephen added, "and I've found some fine specimens. You will see photographs of them out in the shop, after dinner."

A few minutes later, outside in the dusk, Stephen and Margaret led Annette down the garden path to the workshop under the oak tree in the back yard. Mr. Thurston had had the shop built for Stephen because of the boy's talent for wood carving.

When Stephen opened the door, they were greeted by the pleasant smell of wood, varnish, oil, and wax. As they stepped inside, he switched on the electric light.

Annette caught her breath. "Oh, I had no idea it would be such a wonderful place!"

Under four large windows on one side was a long workbench, almost the length of the shop. The machin-

ery, run by electricity, consisted of a circular saw, a scroll saw, lathes for turning wood, a plane, and a sanding belt. There were chisels, hammers, and other hand tools, stacks of lumber, sheets of veneer, drawing-boards, and compasses. On the shelves were paints, varnishes, oils, and stains. Brushes stood in cans of turpentine. The walls were almost covered with photographs and drawings of furniture.

Stephen was proud to be showing the shop to his English cousin. He picked up a piece of smooth, reddish-brown mahogany and a piece of chestnut-colored rosewood and ran his fingers over them fondly. "This mahogany comes from Honduras, and the rosewood is from Brazil," he said.

Then he opened a drawer and removed a few photographs. "I took these with Dad's camera. They're pictures of fine old furniture I've found while scouting around."

Annette studied them closely. "I'm very much interested in photographs like this. I—I have a special reason," she added mysteriously.

This was the first of many happy times in the shop. Since Annette was not to enter school until the fall term, she studied her lessons at home in the mornings. But part of each afternoon was spent with Margaret and Stephen working out in the shop.

One afternoon in June, when school had closed and the

children had the whole summer before them, Stephen came running into the shop. "Good news!" he announced to the girls. "We're going on a scouting trip tomorrow with Dad and Mr. Carr, the head designer at the factory."

"Great!" cried his sister gleefully.

"Ripping!" said Annette.

The next morning Mr. Thurston drove Mr. Carr and the three children to a quiet little village about fifty miles from High Point, where quaint old houses were set far back in the yards, shaded by large trees.

He stopped the car near the drug store, drew a newspaper clipping from his pocket and said, "Here is a recent story about Elmwood, the old Martin Gray home, which was built in this village more than a century ago. Stephen, I want you and the girls to call on Mrs. Gray, and ask her to let you photograph some of her rare old pieces of furniture."

Eagerly Stephen glanced at the article and read the first two paragraphs to the girls. Then he hopped out of the car with the camera and equipment.

Mr. Thurston continued, "Mr. Carr and I have an appointment to do some sketching at the Logan place. We'll all meet in the drug store for lunch."

Stephen and the girls walked down the street to the Gray home which stood in the shade of great elm trees. Stephen led the way up the winding gravel walk, bordered with boxwood, to the stately house with its tall white pillars and wide porch. They walked up the steps, and Stephen gave a brisk pull to the shiny brass bell.

For a few minutes, they stood there waiting. Then the door opened a few inches and a sweet voice asked, "Who's there?"

"It's—well," Stephen hesitated. "Here's a card that will explain us."

"Just a minute," said the voice. "I'll get my glasses."

Annette whispered, "What was on the card?"

"It's Dad's business card," he told her, "and he wrote across it, 'Introducing my son, Stephen.' "

Now, the door opened again—wide, this time—and there stood a gracious old lady. "I am Mrs. Gray," she said, with a smile. "What can I do for you, Stephen?"

Stephen introduced Margaret and his cousin and then explained the purpose of their call.

Mrs. Gray's eyes twinkled. "Well, I must say this is a most unusual request. I have often been bothered by antique hunters who want to buy my rare pieces. But"—she hesitated, "if you only want to take pictures of some of my heirlooms I think that will be fun."

Inviting them in, she ushered them through the hall into the dining room. "Perhaps there will be something here that you would like to photograph," she told Stephen. "These are fine old pieces. The table and chairs came from England before the Revolution."

The boy stopped in front of the mahogany sideboard. He gave a soft whistle. "I've never seen such a handsome Sheraton sideboard!"

As he set up his tripod, the girls examined the sideboard with its slender reeded legs and delicately carved thimble feet.

"This is very beautiful," was Margaret's appreciative remark.

Annette asked, "Did it come from England, too?"

Their hostess was rearranging the white roses in a bowl on the table and did not answer right away. "No," she said slowly. "That was made here in North Carolina

in 1800. I think it matches the other pieces rather well."

With great interest, she watched the boy taking photographs of the front and ends. Then she exclaimed, "You'll be surprised to know, Stephen, that you have just taken pictures of a sideboard made by one of the well-known early cabinet-makers. His name is signed on the back—Isaac Thurston . . ."

"Isaac Thurston!" cried three astounded voices.

"Why, he was our great-great-great grandfather!" said Stephen. "We have a portrait of him at our house."

"And we have one just like it in London," added Annette, while Margaret chimed in, "Oh, oh, what a surprise this will be for Dad!"

"Well, to think that I have Isaac Thurston's great-great-great grandchildren here in my dining room!" said Mrs. Gray. "Now, what else would you care to see? There's a fine Hepplewhite desk in the library."

"Another time, thank you." The boy was folding up his tripod. "We're going to meet Dad at the drug store for lunch."

"Oh, yes, another time, we'd love to see more of your heirlooms," Margaret assured her.

"You're welcome at Elmwood whenever you wish to come, my dears," said Mrs. Gray.

A few minutes later, they were telling Mr. Thurston and Mr. Carr about their wonderful "find," but they did not mention the name of the maker of the sideboard.

"Just wait until you see our pictures," said Stephen with an air of triumph.

The next morning while the girls were at work in the shop, Stephen came bounding in with a large brown envelope. "Here they are!" he announced, proudly spreading out the clear glossy prints on the bench.

Margaret and her cousin examined them with great interest. Then Annette took the pictures to the far end of the shop, where she sat down on a sawhorse, with her back to her cousins. For a long while she examined the prints. Margaret and her brother wondered why she studied them so closely.

"Well, how are the master carvers?" said Mr. Thurston, coming into the shop long in advance of lunch time.

"Fine!" replied his son, laying down the tool he was using. "And here are the prints, Dad. We hope you'll like 'em."

The father looked with interest at the pictures. "What a marvelous Sheraton sideboard!" he exclaimed.

"But guess who made it, Dad?" asked Margaret.— "Great-Great-Great Grandfather Thurston. And Mrs. Gray says that his name is signed on the back!"

Mr. Thurston was delighted. "I'll call on Mrs. Gray, of course, to see if she'll lend us her sideboard to be copied in the factory."

Now, Annette said to her uncle, "I'm so excited, I hardly know how to begin. Margaret and Stephen have probably been wondering why I have shown such special interest in the pictures. Now, I'll tell why." She handed her uncle a dark-blue album which she had been holding behind her back. "Mother sent you these photographs of our dining-room set which was made by Isaac Thurston. I've been hoping to find the same design, and here it is—Mrs. Gray's sideboard!"

Too astonished to speak, Margaret, Stephen, and their father compared the pictures in the album with the new prints. Finally, Mr. Thurston said, "This is a great coincidence, Annette. The designs of the two sideboards are exactly alike, as you say. When Isaac Thurston came over to America, he must have decided to make another dining-room set like the one now in your home in England." Thoughtfully, Mr. Thurston looked down at the three excited young people. "Can you keep a big secret?"

"Yes," they all promised.

"Very well," stated Mr. Thurston. "First, I must call on Mrs. Gray and ask permission to borrow her sideboard so that our chief designer can copy it. We've been planning a new mahogany dining-room set for the market. With Mrs. Gray's Sheraton sideboard made by Isaac Thurston, we can now use Annette's pictures as patterns for the other pieces. I would like to give Mother one of the first sets for a Christmas present. That is the secret you must keep."

"Oh, it's a wonderful secret!" cried Margaret.

The next morning, Mr. Thurston drove to Elmwood, taking the children with him. After he told her the story, Mrs. Gray gladly gave permission to have the sideboard taken to the factory to be copied. Then Stephen and Margaret and Annette helped him move the sideboard out a few inches from the wall to examine the back.

"It's here!" Stephen was gleeful. "It's carved in small letters."

With great curiosity, the others looked. There the name was: *Isaac Thurston*. And the date: *1800*.

Vacation was passing quickly. Annette and her cousins visited Mrs. Gray several times during the summer, and shared with her the secret of the Christmas present.

At last Mr. Thurston told the children they might start their visits to the factory to see the different steps in the making of the new dining-room set.

Mr. Dudley, the superintendent, acted as their guide through the large plant which covered thirteen acres. He showed the great kiln where stacks of rough lumber were being seasoned by heat and moisture regulated from a control room.

They next entered a three-story building where men were operating machines, electrically driven. The children watched boards being sawed into pieces for the different sections of the furniture, and then smoothed on large drums covered with sandpaper. They saw steel plungers punching dowel holes in the sections which were to be joined to other parts by wooden pegs.

But the most remarkable of all the machines were the multiple "master carvers." These were twenty-one feet long and eight feet wide, Mr. Dudley explained, and they carved twenty-five pieces at a time. A man sat at this machine, guiding its movements by tracing a model in front of him which had been made by the head carver.

In the finishing department, the young visitors admired the beautiful, soft finish of the stained and varnished woods, and watched the work being done by machines as well as by hand-rubbing.

"We ship six thousand carloads of furniture a year," said the superintendent. "I think the old master carvers would be pleased to know that our skilled craftsmen are really following in their footsteps. Our multiple carving machinery enables us to make excellent reproductions of their finest handmade furniture for the homes of America."

Months passed before the first complete new dining-room set came off the production line. And now it was Christmas time. School was out for the holidays, and the Thurston children were busy with their shopping. Annette's package, including book ends she had made in the shop, and gifts from all the Thurstons, had been mailed to England.

MASTER CARVER

A holly wreath, tied with red ribbon, was hung on the front door. Ground-pine and mistletoe decorated the living room and hall. In the kitchen, pumpkin and mince pies, cranberry sauce, and other good things were being made. The fruit cake had been made weeks earlier.

The day before Christmas dawned clear and cold. Stephen and a friend brought in a fragrant cedar tree, cut from Mr. Thurston's farm in the country, and set it up in the living room. There were presents to be wrapped. Friends came to call. But the most exciting event of the day for the children was the expected arrival of the new furniture, which was to be delivered at four o'clock. Mrs. Thurston must be out of the house before it came!

At three o'clock, Mr. Thurston telephoned to his wife asking her if she could be ready at three-thirty to go to see the Carrs. Mrs. Thurston said she was very busy; but the children urged her to go and helped her to get ready.

Soon after Mr. and Mrs. Thurston had driven down the street, one of the factory trucks arrived at the door, with the new furniture. Two men came in and removed the old furniture from the dining room and put the new pieces in place. Then the two girls set the table for dinner.

When Mr. and Mrs. Thurston came back a little before six o'clock, everything was ready. The silver candlesticks held red candles, and near one of them was propped a card which read:

Merry Christmas—With hearts full of love from Dad, Stephen, Margaret, and Annette.

"Am I in the wrong house?" asked Mrs. Thurston when she came into the dining room, her eyes wide with astonishment.

"No, you're really in your own home, and this is your Christmas present," said Mr. Thurston, beaming with happiness.

While Mrs. Thurston looked lovingly at each piece, the children, all talking at once, explained about the great secret they had been keeping ever since June.

"To think that I didn't suspect!" she said. "Although I will admit that sometimes I did wonder what certain whispering was about."

In the midst of the excitement, the doorbell rang. Annette's father, his arms filled with packages, had arrived from New York unexpectedly.

As soon as the greetings were over, he was, of course, led into the dining room and told about the surprise.

"I can hardly believe my eyes," he declared, as he looked at the table, the chairs, sideboard, and cabinet, just like those in his home in London.

"The sideboard is the most beautiful one I have ever seen," stated Mrs. Thurston.

"I'm glad you think so," said her husband, "because it happens to have been made by Isaac Thurston!"

"What?" the children shouted together.

"When Mrs. Gray realized how much the old sideboard meant to our family," explained Mr. Thurston, "she agreed to sell it to me. I have had a perfect duplicate made for her."

"My goodness!" said Margaret. "This is the greatest surprise of all, and wasn't Mrs. Gray a dear to sell us her precious heirloom?"

After the evening meal was over, the family sat in the living room, listening to the Christmas carols over the radio.

"Now, if Mother were only here, everything would be perfect," said Annette, wistfully.

"Well, let's listen to the London broadcast," suggested her uncle as he turned the dial. "That will make home seem nearer."

From across the ocean in London, came the sound of Big Ben striking the hour, and the same lovely Christmas carols that had just been sung in America.

From his portrait above the mantel, Great-Great-Great Grandfather Thurston seemed to be smiling down on the happy scene.

Bells of St. Michael's

SOUTH CAROLINA

IT was April in Charleston, South Carolina. The morning air was fragrant with the perfume of flowers. The cardinals were singing their sweet songs. From the shining white steeple of St. Michael's, the old eighteenth-century bells were chiming the quarter-hour. To Jeanne they seemed to be saying, as they did every morning:

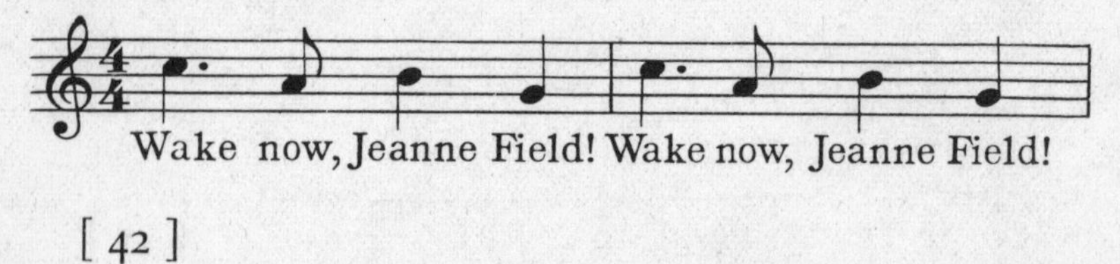

Drowsily Jeanne heard them, but still she snuggled beneath the covering. Then she heard again the bells of St. Michael's:

As the bells chimed eight, Jeanne hopped out of bed. She would have to hurry if she wanted to get to school on time.

Father, Mother, and Andy were already at the table when she came into the sunny dining room. Judy was bringing in the hominy from the kitchen.

"Listen, folks," said Father from behind his newspaper, "the paper this morning is full of the Azalea Festival." He read an item here and there: " 'This year's Azalea Festival promises to outshine the Festivals of other years. Many visitors have already arrived, and hundreds more are expected. Most of the queens and their attendants from the towns and cities of South Carolina are here. Never have the azaleas and other spring flowers been so lovely. The two-century-old Middleton Gardens and the century-old Magnolia Gardens are aflame with color.' "

Mr. Field handed the paper to Jeanne. "Here's the program for the coming week."

"Read it aloud," said Andy, as he poured maple syrup

on a crisp, golden-brown waffle which Judy had just placed before him.

Jeanne started to read: " 'Monday, 4 P.M., Grand Parade; 10 P.M., Ball at Ashley Park. Tuesday, 5 P.M., Street Criers' Contest on the Battery—' Oh, Andy!" she cried, her eyes shining. "Why doesn't Daddy Tennant enter that contest? He's the best street crier in Charleston." And Jeanne softly chanted those familiar words:

"Here's your Daddy Tennant, ma'am.
I got Hoppen John Peas, ma'am!
I got cabbage—
I got yallow turnips, ma'am!
Oh, yes, ma'am."

"That's a good idea," answered Andy. "Let's speak to him about it when he comes home from work this afternoon. He'd get the money prize, if he won."

Jeanne and her brother Andy loved Daddy Tennant. The old Negro lived in the little cottage in the court behind their home. A gate had been cut in the fence, and Jeanne and Andy were constantly running in and out of his yard. Daddy spent his days pushing his little cart of vegetables through the streets. Every day when he came home, he would call: "Come, children, I've got peanuts for you!" And Jeanne and her brother would go running to meet him and listen to his stories.

That afternoon when they heard him rolling his cart

through the court, they rushed across the lawn and slipped through the gate. They sat on the steps of his piazza for their usual daily visit.

"Daddy Tennant," commenced Jeanne, "we think you should enter the Street Criers' Contest next Tuesday. You might win the prize."

"That's just what my Miss Kershaw was telling me this morning," replied Daddy. "But go 'long, children, I could never win a prize. This cart of mine is too ricketty."

Andy and Jeanne glanced at the cart which he had not yet pushed into the shed. As usual, it looked as if it were about to fall apart.

Eagerly Jeanne suggested, "Then you needn't take the cart. You can carry your vegetables in a basket on your head. Please, Daddy—"

"No, child." Daddy Tennant pulled on his pipe thoughtfully. "Where I go, my cart goes."

Andy and Jeanne looked at each other. They had to agree that it wouldn't seem natural to see Daddy Tennant in the Street Criers' Contest without his cart. Through the years he had become a familiar figure on the streets of Charleston. With the wind ruffling his white hair and beard, he would walk slowly along, pushing the little cart—that unpainted, splintery, ricketty-racketty old thing with two wheels that went this way and that way, that way and this way—*squeak, squeak; squeak, squeak.*

"Just this once go without the cart, and enter the contest," pleaded Jeanne.

"Please," added her brother. "We want you to win the prize."

Pulling on his pipe, the old man gazed into space. After a while he remarked quietly: "Albert Conyers told me I could borrow his cart. He's gone to Edisto Island."

Andy jumped to his feet, excitedly. "Daddy, let's go and get it now! Albert's house is just around the corner."

But when they came back with the cart, Jeanne realized it was not right. Although it was sturdy, it was too drab and shabby. While they were examining it, the bells of St. Michael's chimed.

"Oh, Andy!" she cried, and her eyes were twinkling. "The bells are telling me: 'Paint now, Jeanne Field! Paint now, Jeanne Field!' "

Her brother laughed. "Those are mighty convenient bells. I've noticed that whenever you want to do anything very badly, you always say the bells are telling you to do it."

Jeanne laughed. "But seriously, Andy. Let's paint the cart. I want Daddy Tennant to win that prize." She turned to Daddy. "If we fix this cart up, will you enter the contest?" But he wasn't even listening to her; his thoughts were far away.

Andy looked at him, doubtfully. "Jeanne," he said, "usually your ideas are good, but I'm not sure about this one. Anyway, before we can paint this cart we'll have to sandpaper it. Let's go and ask Ben to help us."

Down the street the two children hurried, past the Sword Gate House, surrounded by its high brick walls. Jeanne stopped as she always did to trace with her fingers the old Roman sword and spear wrought into the iron gates. Then she peeped through them, down the avenue of magnolias, at the old house itself.

She liked to picture the time when the Sword Gate House had been a school for girls. In her imagination, she could see her great-great-grandmother, Jeanne de Beaufain, as a schoolgirl, strolling along the flagstone walk under those trees. How often she must have walked beneath those magnolias when the bells of St. Michael's were chiming. Perhaps she had thought that they were calling her name, as they seemed to be doing now: "Jeanne de Beau-fain! Jeanne de Beau-fain!"

"Come on, Jeanne," begged Andy. "We have to go to Ben's and still be home in time for supper. Judy told me she was giving us shrimp pie and corn sticks."

When their playmate, Ben, heard of their plans, he was anxious to help. "I have some yellow and red paint," he said, "and we can buy some apple-green in the morning. We'll get some of that quick-drying paint. Then I'll do the decorating. And if Daddy Tennant doesn't win that prize, I'll eat my hat."

The next morning was Saturday. The three children were gathered in the shed under the old elm tree in Daddy Tennant's yard. First came the sandpapering. Jeanne soon was tired and her arms ached. But she was determined to keep on, since the whole idea was hers.

From time to time she glanced through the gate into the garden where her mother was directing Alex, the yard boy, as he mowed the lawn and trimmed the hedges. Mother, too, was getting ready for the Azalea Festival. She wanted her garden to be lovely when visitors thronged the streets and peeped in at the gates.

In all Charleston, Jeanne thought their garden was the loveliest with its different shades of green, and the pink of the roses and the azaleas, the yellow of the jessamine, and the lavender of the wisteria. In the midst of all this color, was the old white house with its yellow-curtained windows and the yellow jessamine that climbed the piazza rails.

After the sandpapering came the painting. The children gave the cart an even coat of apple-green.

"It'll be dry by afternoon," Ben promised. "Just wait until you see the fancy decorations I'm going to put on." Chuckling, he went home to lunch.

The bells of St. Michael's were ringing four o'clock when the children again gathered in the shed. Daddy Tennant was with them. He sat smoking his pipe and watching Ben work.

At last Ben finished. There was the little cart, brave and beautiful with garlands of red peppers around the sides, bunches of carrots and radishes at the corners, and clusters of tomatoes here and there!

"Oh, boy!" cried Andy. "That looks swell!"

"It's the most beautiful cart in Charleston!" exclaimed Jeanne. "Joe Cole's cart can't compare with this."

Ben considered this a compliment. He knew that Joe had a cart at which people turned to look. Joe was a fish vender, and his cart was in the shape of an ark. It was painted yellow and decorated with red fish. As he went along the streets, he was always followed by his three cats.

"Oh, Daddy!" said Jeanne. "Don't you think the cart looks beautiful?"

The old man rose to his feet, knocked the ashes from his pipe and put it in his pocket. Slowly he strolled over to his cottage.

"I'm sure he likes it," said Andy, "but he just won't say so."

On Monday, the city was crowded with visitors. Andy and Jeanne were as excited as everyone else on the opening day of the Azalea Festival. During school they found it hard to keep their minds on their lessons, and when they came home in the afternoon, they had almost forgotten the cart out in the shed.

The Grand Parade started at four o'clock. Jeanne and her brother and Ben made their way through the crowds and found a place to stand on the curb along the line of the parade. Narrow old King Street was jammed with jolly, carefree people. They milled about the sidewalks, leaned out of office windows, or stood on the housetops, leaning over the low walls along the edges of the roofs.

The street was a mass of color. Flags and pennants were everywhere. Strings of colored lights were strung from pole to pole. Venders walked up and down selling bright-colored balloons. Boy Scouts and policemen were trying to keep the street clear.

Suddenly, strains of music sent tingles up and down Jeanne's back. The parade was approaching, and the band was playing *Dixie!* The three children stood there on the curb, humming the beloved tune.

First, a troop of city and state police came marching by. Then, the band. Next came a detachment of cadets from the Citadel in their gray uniforms with white cross-belts and their tall hats and plumes; then, automobiles with the distinguished visitors.

"The Governor of South Carolina and the Mayor of Charleston are riding in that first car," Andy told Jeanne.

Next came the visiting queens, each riding in a rickshaw, beautifully decorated with spring flowers and drawn by a boy dressed in a Chinese costume.

Music again, and float after float went rolling by while the crowd cheered and clapped. Some of the floats were masses of flowers. One represented a huge pink azalea. Some represented gardens with arbors and lattices; others, plantation scenes with children singing old Southern songs.

There were colonial ladies and gentlemen, and pirates with gold rings in their ears and black patches over their eyes. But the float that brought the loudest applause was the *City of Charleston*. "Miss Charleston," a lovely young woman, sat on a bale of cotton in front of a huge sea shell surrounded by four tall palmetto trees.

"It was the best parade ever!" declared Andy when it was all over. Jeanne and Ben agreed.

Before breakfast the following morning, Jeanne hurried out to the shed to take one last look at the gay little cart, for Daddy Tennant would be gone by the time they returned from school. To her surprise, Andy was there ahead of her.

"Well," he remarked, "we won't see this again until Daddy Tennant comes pushing it up South Battery this afternoon. I know you'll feel proud because you thought up all this."

Just then the bells of St. Michael's chimed eight o'clock, and to Jeanne they seemed to be saying: "Dad-dy Ten-nant! Dad-dy Ten-nant!"

"Oh, I do hope he wins!" she exclaimed. "And something tells me that he will."

Slowly the day passed with St. Michael's chiming the quarter-hours. At last, it was five o'clock, and the three excited children were there on the crowded Battery.

Now a band began to play the *National Emblem March*. Eagerly the children leaned forward as the band came marching toward them. They knew it was the Jenkins Band. As the boys of the band came tramping past, dressed in their red and blue uniforms, Ben said, "It wouldn't seem like the Azalea Festival without that band."

When it reached the judges' stand, the music ceased. There was quiet. Then through a loud speaker, came an announcement:

"Ladies and gentlemen! Girls and boys! You are about to witness the most unique feature of the Azalea Festival—the Street Criers' Contest. Charleston is famous for her street cries. Some have been chanted in this old city for generations. Will everyone remain quiet, please."

Up South Battery came the first street crier pushing his little bright-blue cart piled high with lovely fresh vegetables, and singing over and over again:

"Lady wan'
Sweet peas,
Green cawn,
Red-rose tomatoes,
GREEN CAWN!"

After him, came a tall thin woman balancing on her head a basket of shrimp, and crying:

"Get your raw, raw, raw schimp, ma'am,
You like 'em raw, raw, raw, schimp, ma'am!"

After the shrimp woman, came the crab man pushing his pea-green cart and chanting that cry which the children knew was as much a sign of springtime in Charleston as the song of the cardinal:

"She craib!
She craib!
She craib!"

Next, strode a woman bearing on her head a basket of flowers. Head up, arms by her side, eyes to the front, she walked by in silence. A murmur of admiration rippled through the crowd.

Crier after crier passed. Each was dressed in the clothes he wore every day.

Then the children heard a pleasing voice singing in the distance:

> "Old Joe Cole, good old soul—
> Porgy in the summertime
> An' e whiting in the spring—
> Eight upon a string.
> Don't be late—I'm waitin' at de gate.
> Don't be mad—here's your shad.
> Old Joe Cole, good old soul!"

Along came Joe Cole, pushing his fine yellow cart decorated with its red fish. As always, he was followed by his

three cats. There was a whistling and clapping of hands as he went on his way.

Jeanne's heart sank. She wondered if Joe would win the contest after all.

Then she heard a *squeak, squeak; squeak, squeak*. She turned quickly, and there was the next vender. He was an old man. He walked slowly along pushing his cart, with the wind ruffling his white hair and beard. Astonished, she watched his approach.

He was *not* pushing a little apple-green cart, gay with garlands of red peppers around the sides, and with bunches of carrots and radishes at the corners, and clusters of tomatoes here and there. He was pushing a little unpainted, splintery, ricketty-racketty old thing with two wheels that went this way and that way, that way and this way—*squeak, squeak; squeak, squeak*.

Jeanne turned to her brother in bewilderment. "Brace up," he whispered. "Wait and see what happens."

Strolling along, pushing his cart, Daddy Tennant sang in his mellow voice:

"Here's your Daddy Tennant, ma'am.
I got Hoppen John Peas, ma'am!
I got cabbage—
I got yallow turnips, ma'am!
I got sweet petater,
I got beets,
I got guinney squash!
Oh, yes, ma'am."

The old man's chant was so sweet, there was such a sadness to it, that it captured the hearts of all who heard.

When the parade was over, everybody crowded close to the judges' stand. Andy, Jeanne, and Ben got there just in time to see Daddy Tennant go up the steps to receive a little box from one of the judges. Daddy made a gracious, courtly bow. The crowd began to cheer and call his name.

"Daddy Tennant!" exclaimed Jeanne when she finally got near him. "Where's that cart we painted for you?"

The old man's eyes twinkled. "Where I go, *my* cart goes."

As Jeanne looked into his happy face, she was glad he had done as he wished about using his own cart. But she knew that he would not have entered the contest except for her.

Just then the bells of St. Michael's began chiming in the soft evening air, and they seemed to be saying:

"Well done, Jeanne Field!
Well done, Jeanne Field!"

Thoroughbred

KENTUCKY

"IT'S our last day together, Belle," whispered Annie Laurie sadly. The thoroughbred bay horse on which she was riding nickered as if it understood.

They were following the road that led to the river, at Idle Acres, a big stock farm in Kentucky which belonged to Annie Laurie's father and had been in the Applegate family for many generations. She and Belle had both been brought up on Idle Acres.

"In this filly's veins," Mr. Applegate had told Annie Laurie time and time again, "flows the bluest blood of the turf—back to the great English Leamington, sire of the world-famous Kentucky horses."

Now, when they came to the willows at the water's edge, Annie Laurie slid from the horse's back, and resting her head against Belle's shoulder, began to cry.

"Oh, shucks, I bet it isn't half that bad," said a voice, suddenly.

Startled, Annie Laurie raised her head. She could see no one. Belle, however, had pricked up her ears and was pointing her nose toward a near-by clump of willows on the shore. Seated on a log, with a fishing pole dangling from the crook of one arm, and his bare feet stretched into the rippling water, was a boy.

"Oh, yes, it is!" she retorted. "It's a lot worse than that."

"Why not sit down?" the boy asked.

Picking up Belle's bridle, Annie Laurie walked over to the log under the trees where she left the horse nibbling the willow buds. She sat down on the log.

"No use crying on a day like this," said the boy. Then giving a yank to his fishing pole, he laughed. "I thought I had a trout."

Annie Laurie removed her sandals and thrust her feet into the water. She watched the sunlight dancing on the ripples of the river.

"It's because it is a day like this that makes things seem so—" She was nearly crying again. "What I mean is, if today wasn't so fine, Idle Acres wouldn't look so beautiful, and perhaps I wouldn't feel so bad at the thought of having to give it up."

The boy gave her a sidewise glance. "Why d'you have to?"

Annie Laurie stared gloomily at the water. "Well, somehow folks haven't been buying enough of our horses to make the farm pay."

"Is that all?" laughed the boy. "That's easy to change. All you have to do is raise what folks will buy—like—beef cattle or—

"Beef cattle?" She looked at him pityingly. Of course, he didn't know any better. Then she explained gently. "The bluegrass is for *horses*. Nowhere else do you find the limestone soil that grows such bluegrass as here in Kentucky. That's why our horses are so beautiful. Limestone makes fine bones."

He grinned. "Wouldn't it make fine beef bones, too?"

"Beef bones?" She had to laugh at the thought of sitting there on that log with such an ignorant boy. "Only horses—fine horses—will ever feed in our bluegrass. They're the grandest things in the world. My ancestors thought so, my father thinks so—and so do I," Annie Laurie tossed her head. "All the Applegates have always felt the same way."

"Well," said the boy, "if horses don't pay, you'd better think of something else." He jerked his fishing pole.

"Thought I had a bite that time. If you'll take my advice, you'll tell your father to give up part of his meadows for beef cattle. There's always a market for beef."

Annie Laurie regarded him with sudden interest.

"That's a good idea," she told him, "*part* of the meadows for beef cattle—"

"Sure, it is!" he agreed. "It's my dad's idea."

"The trouble is," said Annie Laurie, "it's too late." She drew her feet from the water to dry them in the sun. "This is our last day at Idle Acres. Tomorrow, the new owner is coming to take it over and we're going to move into the city. We'll miss the bluegrass. We'll miss it terribly."

The boy frowned. "It wasn't such a good idea, after all, was it?"

"Oh, yes, it was," she assured him. "And I thank you just the same—" She paused. "I'm Annie Laurie. What's your name?"

"Henry," said the boy.

He tossed his fishing pole on the shore and began putting on his shoes.

Annie Laurie slipped her feet into her sandals. Then they got up from the log and strolled towards Belle who was still nibbling the willow buds. Henry ran a gentle hand along Belle's velvety neck. "This is the most beautiful horse I ever saw," he said.

"I guess she is," declared Annie Laurie. "She's the

most beautiful horse in Kentucky. She's got the blood of champions. She's won blue ribbons and silver cups. Would you like to ride her?"

"Well—" the boy hesitated. "I'm not much of a rider."

"Oh, you don't have to be afraid of Belle," she assured him. "She won't go fast unless you tell her to."

"Well, all right," decided Henry. "I'd like to see what it's like to ride a horse that's won blue ribbons and silver cups."

Annie Laurie led Belle over to a tree stump so that the boy could mount. Then she handed him the bridle. He clucked at Belle, who, instead of heading toward the

road, stepped daintily across the shore and into the stream to take a drink. She put her head down and down and down.

"Hold on!" Annie Laurie called.

"I'm trying to!" replied the boy, clutching at Belle's mane and digging his knees into her sides.

Annie Laurie knew what was going to happen—and it did. Belle lowered her neck one bit more, and the boy slid over her head and with a loud splash landed in the water. Then Belle calmly took a drink and stepped back to the shore.

Sputtering and gasping, Henry got to his feet. "Did I look funny?" he asked good-naturedly.

"Did you look funny?" Annie Laurie laughed as he came wading toward her with his wet clothes clinging to him. But before she could reply, there was a shout behind her, and she turned to see a group of amused men sitting in a car that had stopped by the trees.

"Sonny!" one of the men called. "Would you mind doing that stunt over again for a movie shot? We'd pay you for it." The man got out of the car and came down to where Henry stood with Annie Laurie and Belle.

"I'd be willing to." The boy grinned. "But I guess Belle will shy away from me now, after that bad start."

"Then it isn't your horse?" the man asked.

"No," replied Henry, removing his shoes to pour out the water. "She belongs to Annie Laurie."

"She's mine until tomorrow." Annie Laurie spoke quietly, as she patted Belle on the shoulder. "Then she'll belong to the man who's bought the farm. She goes with Idle Acres."

"Idle Acres?" the man asked.

"That's the name of the farm," she explained. "The new owner's going to take all the horses."

"Don't look so sad," Henry told her, struggling into his wet shoes. "Perhaps something will happen so you can keep Idle Acres."

"Oh, nothing can happen now," she told him. "It's too late."

The man returned to the car and talked with the other men. When he joined the children again, he said to Annie Laurie, "Can you ride?"

Could she ride? Annie Laurie didn't know how to answer such a question. She'd been riding since she was four years old. "Well—" she hesitated. Then she added with her eyes twinkling, "I can a little."

Eagerly she stepped on the tree trunk and took the horse's bridle. Belle dipped her head, and catching her mane, Annie Laurie was on the horse's back in a jiffy. Then across the road and into the bluegrass meadow. Now leaping the fence and up the rise of ground with nothing ahead but sky and white clouds.

The last day at Idle Acres! sang the wind in her ears. Down, down, down the meadow and once more over the fence. Now, again on the river road, Belle's hoofs seemed to pound out the words: *The last day at Idle Acres!* Then, under the willow trees and in a cloud of dust, Annie Laurie and Belle slid to a sudden stop right beside the car.

The men clapped their hands, and Henry cheered.

"That settles it," declared the man who had asked her if she could ride. "Browning, we have something here," he said to the man behind the wheel.

"Yes," Mr. Browning replied. "We've looked all over Kentucky for just this, Bates." He turned to Annie Laurie. "Young lady, how would you and your horse like to be in a motion picture?"

"You mean—the movies?" exclaimed Henry.

"Oh, I'd love it if Belle could be in a picture," answered Annie Laurie. "I'd love everybody in the world to see Belle. But as for me—well, I won't be around here after today."

"Perhaps it can be arranged somehow," said Mr. Bates. "Is your father at home?"

"Oh, yes! He's up at the house. Just follow the road—you can't miss it. It's white with a wide veranda and pillars, and a turf track in front."

Mr. Bates got back into the car. "Are you going our way, son?" he asked Henry.

"No, I'm spending the day at the Martins' place," replied the boy, picking up his fishing pole.

"Oh, please go that way first," Annie Laurie told Mr. Browning. "He ought to get out of those wet clothes."

"Hop in, son." Mr. Browning opened the door. "It'll give us a chance to talk about your stunt in the picture."

"I'll be over to see you before you go," Henry assured Annie Laurie as he drove off with the men.

Thoughtfully, she rode home, taking a short cut across the meadow so that she could speak to her father before the men got there. She left Belle at the stable and ran to the house. Mr. Applegate met her at the door.

"There are some moving-picture men here!" she exclaimed. "And what do you think? They want Belle to be in a picture—they want me to be in it, too, but—I said I wouldn't be here." Her chin quivered.

"No tears, daughter," said her father, putting his arm around her. "We mustn't spoil our last day at Idle Acres." He looked beyond her to where the drive curved in from the river road. "Are those your moving-picture men?"

Annie Laurie turned. "Yes, here they are now. They're coming to see you. Oh, I hope Belle can be in the picture! And when we get to the city, and—and are homesick for the bluegrass—maybe we could see her on the screen."

There was the car now in front of the veranda. Mr. Bates jumped out and introduced himself, followed by Mr. Browning and the others. After a few words, Mr. Applegate invited them inside, and Annie Laurie sat down on the steps to wait.

Beyond the stables, the bluegrass was bending in the breeze, and she thought of what Henry had said about giving up part of the meadows for beef cattle. If only she had known him before that last day at Idle Acres, she thought. Perhaps they might have persuaded her father to raise some beef cattle.

After a while, the men came out on the veranda again.

"I tell you, there's nothing I can do about it," Mr. Applegate was saying. "It's entirely up to the new owner. But I'll be pleased to show you around."

Tucking her hand into her father's, Annie Laurie tagged along.

They visited the stables where the timothy and bluegrass hay, and clover and alfalfa from the overflowing lofts sent out a fragrance through the warm air. The dust danced in the long ribbons of sunlight that sifted through the cracks in the walls. Over the low rails of the whitewashed stalls, the horses looked at them—the bay, brown, and sorrel horses that Annie Laurie knew and loved.

Mr. Applegate led his guests out of the stables to show them the rest of the farm.

"Idle Acres has been in the Applegate family since the Revolutionary War when my ancestors fought in the campaign of George Rogers Clark," he told them.

"How have you managed to keep everything looking like an old-fashioned plantation?" one of the men asked.

Mr. Applegate explained, "The property has always

been inherited with the understanding that any repairs must follow the original plans."

They walked past the white fences with their criss-crossed bars between the top and bottom rail. Some of the stable boys were dipping wide brushes into buckets of whitewash, giving the finishing touches to the paddock fence. They looked up and smiled at the visitors.

In the meadow beyond, brood mares stood among the pink clover and bluegrass, nibbling at tender shoots, or nuzzling their little awkward colts wobbling on shaky, nobby legs.

On the way back, they stopped at the Turf House. Here, the great fireplace, where a big log always burned in cool weather, yawned black and empty. Hanging on the walls were paintings or photographs of generations of horses raised on the Applegate farm. A glass case was filled with gold-lettered ribbons of blue, red, yellow, and purple—honors won at fairs and racing meets. On the wide, hand-hewn mantel stood a row of silver cups engraved with the names of some of the thoroughbred prize-winners from Idle Acres.

The men spent the day there on the farm, and Mr. Applegate invited them to stay for early supper and meet the new owner who was going to drop in that evening.

While they lingered at the long candle-lit supper table, Mr. Bates and his friends told more of their plans for the picture.

If they could come to terms with the new owner, the picture would be taken there at Idle Acres. Annie Laurie wouldn't be expected to act at all—all she would have to do would be to ride, and stay near Belle.

"The idea is," Mr. Bates explained to Annie Laurie, "that, in the movie, you are the childhood memory of the grown-up heroine who still lives on her ancestral plantation."

There was a heavy step on the veranda just then, and the conversation ended before Annie Laurie could ask about Henry's part in the picture. Mr. Applegate went to the door and welcomed Mr. Slater, the new owner.

Annie Laurie slipped outside into the soft blue haze, which is dusk in Kentucky. She sat down on the top step and leaned back against one of the tall white pillars, trying not to feel too hopeful about Mr. Slater.

"Hello!" a cheerful voice greeted her. Surprised, she saw Henry coming up the steps. "I told you I'd be over," he said.

"The new owner is inside," she whispered excitedly. "The movie men are going to see if he'll let them use Idle Acres. They think he will, if they offer him enough. Oh, I do want Belle to be in that picture so the whole world can see her. They want me in it, too, and I can be—if only Mr. Slater will agree and let us stay on here long enough."

"They want me in it, too," said Henry. "D'you think Belle will let me slide over her head again into the river?"

They both laughed at that. For a while, they didn't talk at all, wondering what was being decided in the house. They heard voices, low and serious. Then came the voice of Mr. Slater, "You keep Idle Acres, Mr. Applegate," he was saying, "and I'll pick up that option on the Martins' farm down the road. And after the picture's been taken, I'll help you get started with beef cattle—just part of the meadows, you know—"

"Beef cattle!" exclaimed Annie Laurie, clutching Henry by the sleeve. "Part of the meadows for beef cattle? Why, that's just what you said this morning!" Before Annie Laurie could say anything else, the men were coming out on the veranda.

"Then I'll see you at the lawyer's office tomorrow," said Mr. Slater, shaking hands with Mr. Applegate. "Your bluegrass is made for thoroughbreds. But if you keep part of the meadows for beef cattle, you'll have something you can always count on. Come on, Henry. Let's get going. Good-night, Mr. Applegate."

Mr. Applegate walked down the steps with him while Henry ran ahead and hopped into the car standing in the driveway. "Come around often, Henry," he invited the boy. "You'll always be welcome at Idle Acres."

So Henry was Mr. Slater's son! Annie Laurie was too astonished to say anything.

After the car had driven off into the deepening dusk, she walked slowly away from the group on the veranda.

She followed the turf track as far as the pasture and found Belle there by the gate.

"Idle Acres is ours—for keeps, Belle," she said, climbing onto the fence where she sat down with her arm around the mare's neck. "And you're going to be in the movies—and the whole world will see how beautiful you are!"

Together they watched the dark settle down over the bluegrass.

Then Annie Laurie noticed the evening star, and as was her custom, she began:

"Star light, star bright,
First star I've seen tonight,
I wish I may, I wish I might—"

She stopped short. There was no use wishing, for all of her wishes had come true!

Singing Fiddle

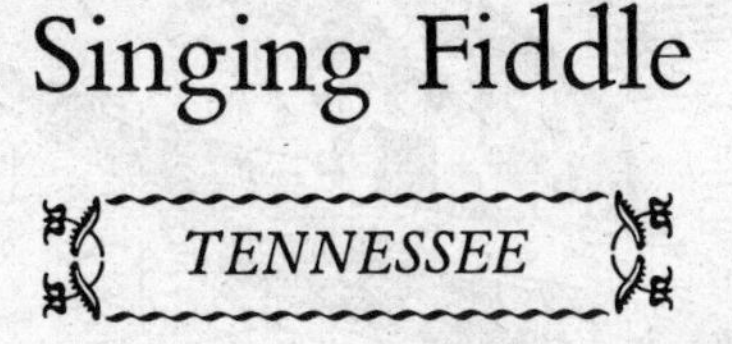

"IT'S seven o'clock!" Gramp Tolliver called from the porch in front of his store. The sun had dropped behind the mountain. The coolness of the June night had settled down.

Gramp Tolliver's store was the only store in the little town, which nestled in a valley of the Great Smokies in Tennessee.

The store always smelled of molasses, corn meal, salt pork, coffee, and cheese. Saddles, harness, pots, and tubs hung on the walls. On the shelves were bolts of calico and gingham, shoes, men's work shirts, trousers, and hats. There was a glass jar of candy sticks on the counter. A wood stove stood in the center of the store, and on a table in a corner was Gramp's radio.

"Isn't it time you started, boy?" Gramp called again.

"I'm almost ready!" Judson's voice came from one of the two rooms behind the store where he and Gramp lived. The furniture was plain, and rag rugs covered the scrubbed floors of split logs.

Jud was thirteen years old and a great help to his grandfather. He worked the acre of ground with a plow

and old Noggin, the mule, and planted the corn and the vegetables. He helped in the store, too, and he was good at keeping house.

Gramp Tolliver was sitting on the porch, carving a piece of red cedar into a frog. Samson, his old hound, was stretched at his feet. The dog's tail thumped on the boards as Judson appeared at the door with his fiddle case tucked under his arm.

Jud picked up the lantern from the nail at the side of the door. "You won't feel lonesome, Gramp?"

The old man studied his carving. "Shucks, no. Have a good time at the party."

"Thanks." Judson walked off into the dusk, swinging

the lantern, which he would need later when coming home. He held the fiddle case carefully. Inside, was the fine old violin which had been in the Tolliver family for a long time. His grandfather had given it to him three years before. The boy loved that fiddle.

Up the road a little way, lived the Simms family. Their house looked yellow with the honeysuckle climbing up one side. Behind it the farm lay tip-tilted on the mountainside.

Jud stopped at the path that led to the door, and whistled. Mrs. Simms came to the front window. "Lethie will be right out!" she called.

Mrs. Simms was a very kind neighbor to Mr. Tolliver and his grandson. She had hung the red-and-white checked curtains at the windows of their rooms behind the shop, and had tucked the goose-feather cushion in the big chair. On Saturdays, she sent Lethie over with some hot corn bread or a pie.

Now the door of the Simms' house opened and closed, and twelve-year-old Lethie came down the path. Her two tight braids hung over her shoulders, and she wore a blue print dress.

"Did you practice?" she asked eagerly.

"All afternoon," Judson replied, "out on the big rock back of the store."

"I practiced, too," she said as they walked up the road toward the school.

Lethie was carrying a musical instrument of wood with three wire strings. Mr. Tolliver had made it for her that past winter. She had gone to the store to buy cheese and had stayed to sing him an old ballad of twenty verses that she had just finished learning.

"If you're so good at singing ballads," he had told her, "you ought to have something to play at the same time. I'll make you a dulcimer (dul′se mer)."

She loved the old ballads that had been brought into these mountains long ago by people who had come from far places across the sea to make their homes here. These folks from England, Ireland, Scotland, and other countries, who had settled in the mountains, had handed down their songs by memory from father to son to grandson. Some families wrote the words down and kept them in a "ballad box." The Simms family had done this, and that was why Lethie knew so many of the songs of long ago.

That evening, the large room in the school was filled with the sound of voices and laughing. Jud and Lethie found that most of their friends had already come. This was the last party of the season, because school would be over in another week.

Jud tuned his fiddle. Then he jumped up on a table that had been pushed against the wall. He tucked his fiddle under his chin. Young folks and grown-ups lined up for the square dances. Everybody that side of the mountain, and from over and beyond, liked to dance when Jud Tolliver played his fiddle.

"What'll it be?" he called out, looking down on the happy faces.

"Weev'ly Wheat!" piped up a voice. That was old Mrs. King. She always asked for *Weev'ly Wheat.*

Judson played the first bar when the notes were drowned out in a clamor for *Sourwood Mountain.* Down came the bow on the strings. Swaying as he played, he sang the words along with the dancers:

"Chickens are crowing on Sourwood Mountain,
Hey did-dy, ump did-dy, id-dy um day!
So many pretty girls I can't count 'em,
Hey did-dy, ump did-dy, id-dy um day!"

Mr. Dunne, the freight agent from the railway station, was calling out the figures for the dances. Now he shouted above the sound of voices and shuffling feet:

"Rights and lefts are what we're after,
Change those hands and step a little faster!"

As he played, Judson sang: "My true love is a sunburnt daisy!"

And at once the dancers joined in:

"She won't work, and I'm too lazy—
Hey did-dy, um did-dy ay!"

While his bow traveled back and forth across the strings, Jud often looked down at Lethie and nodded at her while she danced.

As he fiddled, he saw Miss Perry, his teacher, down there among the dancers. She smiled at him. It was she who had taught him all he knew about music. He had learned quickly, putting his whole heart into the lessons. "He has talent," she had told Gramp. "I'll help him all I can."

After a while, everybody was breathless from so much dancing, and they all sat down to rest on the benches.

"Sing us a ballad, Lethie!" Mr. Dunne called out. Everyone clapped and looked at the girl in blue with the pigtails.

Jud hopped down from the table, and helped Lethie up. He handed her the dulcimer, and lifted up a chair for her to sit on. The folks kept very still. They knew that Lethie had a soft voice, and they wanted to hear every word.

She drew her small, sun-tanned fingers across the three strings. There was a humming sound, like the hum of insects; it was just the right accompaniment for old ballads sung in a childish voice. Stroking the strings, Lethie sang very slowly:

"Oh, where have you been, Lord Randal, my son?
Oh, where have you been, my handsome young man?

I've been to the greenwood, Mother. Make my bed soon,
For I'm wearied with hunting, and fain would lie
down."

When she had finished the words, she continued to draw her fingers over the strings. Then she sang again:

"There's the fairest lady standing yonder
That my two eyes did ever see;
She wears gold rings on every finger,
And on one finger she wears three."

Then Lethie sang the long ballad of twenty verses that had so pleased Mr. Tolliver. Somewhere in the middle,

she stopped playing and Jud's violin came in, oh, so softly, that folks could hardly hear it. They did not speak for a while when the ballad was over; it seemed a shame to start talking after music like that.

Later in the evening, Jud lit his lantern, and he and Lethie walked away from the party. Up the road they stopped to listen to the sounds of the night around them —the humming of insects, frogs croaking, a bird's cry, the shivery whimper of a young owl, and the rustling of the wind through the trees on the mountainside. The boy took out his fiddle and played, and Lethie heard the sounds of the night all over again in his music.

"Oh!" she exclaimed, happily. "That was beautiful, Jud. I heard everything, just like it really is—"

"It isn't good enough yet." He put the fiddle back in its case. They started along the road again. "It needs a melody, Miss Perry says. We're working on that now. She's taught me so much, Lethie, and I'm working and practicing as hard as I can so she'll be proud of me. We're writing the notes down on music paper now. We want to call it the *Song of the Mountain,* but I've got to learn an awful lot more before I can ever finish it right. I reckon it would take a heap of money for me to learn what I want to know about music."

Lethie said promptly, "I wish I had a heap of money. I'd give every penny of it to anybody who'd help you get the *Song of the Mountain* right."

It was the day after school had closed for the summer. Samson, the hound dog, was stretched out on the front porch of the store. Mr. Tolliver sat there carving a dogwood blossom from a piece of cedar. Lethie was watching him. It was Saturday, and Mrs. Simms had sent her over with a huckleberry pie.

"If a pin could be fastened to the back of that flower you're carving," said Lethie, "it would make a brooch for a lady's dress, or it would look nice in her hair—and you could sell it." She was thinking of the money Judson needed for his music lessons.

"Humph," grunted Mr. Tolliver. "Folks come here to buy molasses, and corn meal, and—" He stopped speaking because the dog's tail was thumping on the boards.

"What a lovely bit of carving!" exclaimed a pleasant voice.

Lethie and Gramp turned. A lady was coming up the steps. Standing in front of the store was an open car which had rolled up so quietly that they had not heard it. The man at the wheel smiled at them.

Mr. Tolliver stood up. "What can I do for you, ma'am?" Snapping his knife shut, he tossed the piece of carving into the trash box. He had thrown there many other things which he had made during idle moments.

"May I buy some plain crackers and cheese for our lunch?" she asked, glancing at the box where the carved flower had been tossed.

Lethie stepped inside with Gramp and took a box of crackers from a shelf, while Gramp sliced the cheese and weighed it. Soon the lady had the purchases under her arm, and had gone down the steps.

"You folks here in the mountains can make such lovely things," she remarked. "Why don't you send them down to the shops in the cities? People are glad to pay good prices for mountain craft—bedspreads, hooked rugs, baskets, carving. The folks the other side of the mountain send their things. Why don't you start doing it?"

Samson thumped his tail on the boards as if he thought that was a splendid idea. But Gramp just drawled, "Pshaw. We're not much on—"

"Here's my name and address." The lady handed a card to Lethie. "If you should hear of anyone who *does* want to send such things to sell, please write to me."

She was so cheery and friendly that Gramp stepped over to the trash box and took out the dogwood flower. He dusted it off and handed it to her. "You can have this thing, if you fancy it, ma'am."

After the car had driven away, Lethie glanced at the card. The lady's name was Mrs. Rockwell and she lived in Nashville. Lethie ran to the back garden where Judson was working. She showed him the card and told him what Mrs. Rockwell had said.

"We could send a few things to her, just as samples," Lethie suggested. "My new hooked rug, and one of

Mom's patch quilts, and I've kept lots of Gramp's whittlings. He doesn't know it, but I have. We could send a box off right away, and if Mrs. Rockwell likes them, we'll go to see all the folks around here and ask if they want to sell things that *they* make."

"We could start a regular business," Judson said thoughtfully. "I'll take care of the money when it comes, and give it out to the folks."

"But some of it will be for you," declared Lethie. "Pop and Gramp can figure out what part should be yours."

Judson looked off at the green shoulder of the mountain rising the other side of the road. "I could put it toward my music lessons."

Lethie knew he was thinking of the *Song of the Mountain*.

That evening, the three Simms came down to the store and talked things over with Mr. Tolliver and his grandson. They all decided that the plan was a good one. Then on Monday, the box of samples was packed up with Mrs. Simms' prettiest quilt (the Double Wedding Ring pattern), Lethie's new hooked rug, and an assortment of Gramp's carvings. Mr. Simms drove down to the baggage office with it. It was on its way to Mrs. Rockwell!

Then came long days of waiting, wondering if the things would sell. Finally, in the middle of the summer, the letter came for Gramp. Mrs. Rockwell's name and address were in the upper left-hand corner of the en-

velope. Judson brought it in from the box on the post in front of the store. Lethie was there; her mother had sent her over for some molasses. Gramp seemed to take forever opening his knife to slit the envelope. When the letter was unfolded, there, all typed out plainly, was the good news:

Dear Mr. Tolliver,

The things you sent are all sold. Shops in Nashville, Memphis, and Chattanooga want your mountain craft. Do send as much as you can find. Enclosed is my check for the things already sold.

Sincerely,

Alicia T. Rockwell

And there it was, a blue check, for much more money than they had expected!

"Humph," grunted Mr. Tolliver while the children jumped up and down with excitement. And he sat right down and began to carve a small figure of an old hound dog from a piece of cedar.

The next morning, riding old Noggin, Jud and Lethie set out on their search for mountain craft. Mrs. Simms waved to them as they passed the house.

They stopped first at Grandma Suggs'. It was difficult to make Grandma understand what they wanted because she was deaf. She put her hand behind her ear, and shouted, "Hey? You want a basket? What do you want with it? Hey? Yes, the place is full of baskets, but I don't sell them!"

After a while, they got her to understand that they could help her sell any number of her beautiful honey-suckle-vine baskets to shops in the cities. She was very pleased. "I'll set right to work," she said.

Farther up the road was the Fosters' house. When Jud and Lethie had explained to Mrs. Foster why they had come, she declared promptly, "I'll be proud to piece some quilts. My girls make pretty fans of hickory splints. We'll get some of them ready."

Then Noggin trudged into a dip in the road, and up again to where it led to the Tracys'. The Tracy family had a spinning wheel and a loom. For years, they had spun their own yarn, dyed it with mountain herbs, and woven it into coverlets of many patterns. Mrs. Tracy and her sister liked the plan and would start at once weaving coverlets to sell. They would tell the Bartons who had a loom, too.

"Where next?" Lethie asked, as the mule headed up the road which was growing steeper.

"McCarthy's place," replied Judson.

A little while later, they came to the swinging bridge made of logs chained together and fastened to stumps on either bank of the mountain stream. The narrow bridge swayed as Noggin plodded across. Below, the water lapped over the rocks and carried along twigs and leaves, and in the ripples the sunshine danced like gold pieces.

Jem McCarthy was standing in his doorway. When Judson explained about the plan to sell mountain craft, Jem fell right in with the idea. "My grandsire, and my great, great grandsire, too, made pottery," he told the children. "The old potter's wheel is out in the shed. I turn out a bowl now and then just to keep my hand in practice. Yes, I'll be glad to make some pottery to sell."

Riding home down the road, Lethie and Judson did not speak as they listened to the sounds around them,—the wind in the trees, the melody of bird notes, and the song of the stream.

That evening, Jud wrote to Mrs. Rockwell and reported the outcome of that first search for mountain craft.

He told her what he was going to do with his share of the profits from the sales, and about his violin and Miss Perry's kindness in teaching him music.

So, the young folks there in the mountain valley were carding, or combing, cotton, flax, and wool as their grandmothers and their great-grandmothers had done. The steady hum of spinning wheels, twisting the soft carded rolls into yarn, was now heard again in the houses along the mountain road as it had not been heard for many years. The smaller children roamed fields and woods, gathering herbs to make dye for the yarn.

Then came the busy *th-wack, th-wack, th-wack* of looms weaving the brightly-colored yarn into coverlets of various patterns: Rose in the Wilderness, Tennessee Trouble, and Soldier's Return.

Quilting frames were set up outdoors under the trees on pleasant days. The women and girls came from up the mountain and from over and beyond to help set in the quilting stitches.

There was weaving of rag rugs, too. And there was more carving than had been done for many a day, as Mr. Tolliver and some of his friends spent part of their evenings at the store, whittling.

All this meant that it was the beginning of a busy, happy time along the mountain road. The busiest and happiest person of all was Judson Tolliver. He helped everywhere. He mended spinning wheels, and gathered

honeysuckle vines. He carried the finished articles down to Gramp's to pack them up in boxes for shipping to Mrs. Rockwell in Nashville.

Sometimes there were parties and dances at different houses. Jud played his fiddle and Lethie sang while she drew her fingers over the three strings of her dulcimer. Folks never knew what she would sing because she knew so many ballads.

But the song that everyone liked best of all was the old ballad of twenty verses, where she stopped playing somewhere in the middle, and Jud's violin came in, oh, so softly, that folks could hardly hear it.

The plan of sending mountain craft to Mrs. Rockwell was a wonderful success. Judson kept careful account of the sales and paid folks their profits. He was very proud of his own share. His grandfather gave Jud what money the carving brought, and so the boy had more money for music lessons than he had dared to hope for.

"I'm going to take regular lessons from Miss Perry, and pay her for them," Jud explained to Lethie the last Saturday before school opened. She had been sent over with an apple pie.

"And you can learn a lot more about music—" She did not have time to mention the *Song of the Mountain,* for Mr. Tolliver came in with a letter addressed to Judson. A letter, enclosing a check, had come from Mrs. Rockwell the day before. As the boy opened the envelope, he wondered why she had written again so soon. Now he and Lethie and Gramp read the words:

Dear Jud,

I have written to Miss Perry about your taking violin lessons this fall and winter, in addition to the work in music with her.

I have arranged with a school in Knoxville for you to be given a lesson every Saturday morning. You can easily make the trip by bus, returning home in the afternoon. Miss Perry will tell you more about it when she returns.

Your sincere friend,

Alicia T. Rockwell

"Humph," grunted Mr. Tolliver as he picked up a piece of cedar from the woodbox by the stove and started to whittle a little fiddle.

From outside, came the song of the mountain. Judson and Lethie looked at each other. Now they *knew* that someday Judson would draw those beloved sounds from his violin.

The Cotton-Picking Contest

GEORGIA

THE August sun was sending long slanting rays across the cotton lands of middle Georgia. Evening was on its way.

Jimmy and Patricia Archer were walking along the dirt road between the white fields of cotton that stretched for miles on either side. The cotton bolls were wide open at this season of the year. Between the long rows were the cotton pickers, each with a gray-white canvas bag partly full of the fluffy white cotton.

Jimmy Archer picked cotton on his father's land part of the day. But he worked only until noon because his parents did not like him to work under the broiling heat of the afternoon sun. So, after the midday meal, he did odds and ends of farm jobs, and also had some time to play. Today, he and his sister, who was eleven and just two years younger than he, had gone swimming at a neighbor's, half a mile up the creek. Now they were coming home, swinging their wet bathing suits.

"I can't understand where Pal was when we left the house," said Jimmy. "He always comes when we whistle, and he always goes swimming with us."

"I guess he just didn't hear us whistle," replied Patricia.

"Well, I'll be glad to get home and see if he's there," said her brother.

Now, they talked about the bountiful cotton crop which the fields were bearing, and Jimmy made a rough estimate of how much he was going to earn from his father, picking cotton this year.

Then he said thoughtfully, "I wonder who'll win in the cotton-picking contest?"

"Tom will, of course," Patricia replied. "He's done it for three years now and, of course, he will again."

Tom Stevens was one of the Negro cotton pickers. He was a fine worker of about thirty-eight who lived in a rented house on the Archers' land. He worked for Mr. Archer, and also cultivated his own small farm.

"Yes, I'm sure Tom will win again," Jimmy agreed. "I certainly want him to."

Patricia said, "I do, too."

"There never was another cotton picker like Tom," added her brother. "I guess he can beat anybody in Georgia."

The children had now reached their home. They turned into the path, bordered with petunias, that led to the big white house. When their mother heard them at the front door, she came out of the living room to greet them. "Hello! Have you had a good swim?"

"Oh, yes," Jimmy assured her. Then he asked quickly, "Has Pal come home yet?"

Mrs. Archer replied, "No, your dog hasn't shown up. I can't imagine what's keeping him. Why don't you children go out and call him again?"

Jimmy and his sister hurried out the back door, and whistled loudly again and again. But their beloved wire-haired terrier did not come running as he usually did.

"Oh, dear, I do wonder where he is—" began Patricia.

Then they saw Tom Stevens coming up the side road. He was carrying something in his arms, and they could see that it was their dog.

"Tom!" the children called, running out to the road to meet him.

"What's the matter with Pal?" Jimmy cried. "Where was he?"

"What's happened to him?" asked Patricia. "You've got his leg tied up!"

Tom assured them, "Oh, he's safe now. But he wasn't when I found him. He was caught in a trap that someone had set down in the gully at the side of the road."

"A trap! Gosh!" exclaimed Jimmy, stroking Pal's head. The dog licked his hand lovingly, and then Patricia's as she stroked him, too.

"Is he badly hurt?" she asked.

Tom said, "His leg is broken. But I knew how to fix it. I had a piece of rag in my pocket, and I made splints out of sticks. I think his leg will set right."

"Oh, thank you, Tom," said the boy.

Patricia thanked him, too. "I guess you've saved Pal's life," she added.

Tom smiled at the Archer children. "He's a fine dog." He transferred Pal to Jimmy's arms. As he did so, he had to use his right hand, and he flinched with pain.

"What's the matter?" Jimmy asked. "Did you hurt your hand?"

Tom replied, "When I was pulling myself and Pal up out of that gully, I slipped and fell. Guess I twisted it some."

"Oh!" cried Patricia. "You hurt yourself, rescuing our dog!"

"You certainly are a good friend of ours," Jimmy declared. "We're so sorry you hurt yourself. Can we do anything for your wrist?"

Tom said no, and he'd better be going.

But the children would not let him go. They insisted that he come to the house and let their mother see his wrist. Finally, he agreed. A half hour later, he went off to his own house with his forearm and wrist supported in a sling which Mrs. Archer had made for him.

When Mr. Archer came in a little before suppertime, the children told him what had happened, and they all talked the matter over.

"How's Tom going to win the cotton-picking contest this year?" Patricia asked suddenly with great concern.

Her brother suggested, "Maybe his wrist will get well in time. Do you think it will, Dad?"

"I don't know," replied Mr. Archer a little doubtfully.

Patricia said, "We'll have to *make* his wrist well."

"I do wish we could do something," said Mrs. Archer.

"Well," said Mr. Archer, "I'm driving to town to-morrow on business. I'll take Tom along and let Dr. Innis examine his wrist."

The others were pleased with his suggestion. Then they all had supper, feeling somewhat relieved.

The next morning, Mr. Archer and Tom drove to

town in the car as planned. When they returned, the children and Mrs. Archer came out on the porch to meet them.

"What did Dr. Innis say?" Patricia asked, eagerly.

"Well," Tom told her, "he bound up my wrist some more, and made this new sling. But he wouldn't say whether it would be well in time for the cotton-picking contest over at Byrnes' place."

"Oh," the children groaned.

Mr. Archer explained, "The doctor said that if Tom didn't use his arm at all, the wrist might be entirely well by then. But he also said that if he kept on using it right along, even a little, he couldn't promise anything about it."

Jimmy said quickly, "Then, of course, you mustn't use your arm at all, Tom. You've got to be in the contest."

"Of course, you have to," declared Patricia.

"Well, I sure would like to," admitted Tom, smiling at the eager children. "But I don't see how I can rest my arm all the time. I have to look after myself, you know. Living alone as I do, I have to do my own housework. Then, there's my farm work, too—"

Jimmy and his sister both answered at the same time. "We'll come and help you!" said the boy. "We'll do all that has to be done!" said Patricia.

Tom protested. But Mr. and Mrs. Archer finally persuaded him to let the children help.

"We'll begin right away," Jimmy said. "It's almost noon. We'll bring your lunch to you in a basket in a few minutes."

"And don't you do a thing in the meantime," Patricia begged him.

Tom smiled broadly. "All right," he agreed.

In the following days, the children were very busy. Every morning they went to Tom Stevens' little house with food from their kitchen. They took turns doing the housework, feeding his chickens and his pig, hoeing and weeding his small vegetable patch, and doing other jobs.

In this way, Tom did not have to use his arm, and his wrist improved steadily. It was quite well a week before the picking contest. Then he began to use it a little every day.

The day of the contest arrived! Everybody for miles around drove to the Byrnes' place where it was to be held that year. They came in cars, old and new, in wagons, and some on horseback and on bicycles.

On the west side of the cotton field there was a grove of oak trees in a grassy meadow, and below that was the creek. As the hour for the contest approached, the grove became quite crowded. Here, the spectators settled themselves, as well as the committee in charge, and the men who made up the small band. The picnic baskets were set in the shade of the trees, and bottles of milk and soft drinks were placed in the shallow water at the edge of the creek to keep cool.

Lined up at the side of the field, were the cotton pickers who were going to race with each other to see who could get the most cotton in his sack in the time allowed. The straps of their long, gray-white sacks were slung across their shoulders so that the open top was under the left arm.

Now, Mr. Byrnes, who headed the Contest Committee, gave the signal and the pickers "were off"! In the grove, the band began to play, and the spectators stood there in the shade, watching the contestants crouched between the long rows. The Archers, of course, had their eyes particularly on Tom. Was his wrist really strong enough? Would he be up to his best speed?

Patricia said weakly, "Jimmy, maybe he shouldn't have tried. It would be better if he'd never entered the contest, than if he should be beaten."

"He wanted to be in it," Jimmy reminded her. "Now, we'll just have to wait and see what happens."

Already, Tom had moved some distance off, down his cotton row. Far beyond him, in the large sunny field, the rows all seemed to come together because of the distance. It was a long time before he turned at the other end and worked his way back toward the spectators.

Now, he was approaching the grove. With swift and sure movements of his hands, he pulled the fluffy cotton from the dry bolls. The people in the grove watched him with admiration. The Archers felt hopeful. Still, victory was not certain, for several of the other pickers seemed as expert as he.

After a while, he had again passed far down a cotton row, and Jimmy and Patricia could not distinguish him from the rest of the pickers.

The morning passed. The time of the contest was up! Some of the pickers were approaching the home end of the field, Tom among them. Mr. Byrnes signalled to a member of the band who stood up and blew loudly on his trumpet. That was the signal for the pickers to stop their work. They came toward the grove where the scales were, and the sacks would be weighed.

"Come on," Jimmy whispered to Patricia. "Let's get as near as we can." By hurrying, they secured places directly in front of Mr. Byrnes and the committee.

Now the weighing began. The families, friends, and employers of the contesting pickers stood about talking and speculating. Finally, the last sack was weighed.

Then Mr. Byrnes signalled for silence. There was great suspense while he studied the piece of paper upon which he had written all the records.

"Tom Stevens has won the cotton-picking contest again!" he announced. "He picked two pounds more than any of the others. Last year, he won by a larger margin, but this year he had an accident and sprained his

wrist. This is the fourth consecutive year that Tom has held his place as the champion of the cotton-picking contest here in this region. I guess we can say he's pretty good!"

A cheer went up from the crowd, and the heartiest voices were those of Patricia and her brother. From the Archers' car at the side of the grove, came a dog's happy bark. It was Pal.

Tom stood among the pickers beaming with pleasure.

He said, "I'm glad I won, Mr. Byrnes. I'm mighty proud. I tell you honestly though, I never could have won this year if it hadn't been for the Archers—and especially Jimmy and Patricia."

Mr. Byrnes smiled. "I heard about your sprained wrist, and how the Archer children helped you with the work on your place until it was well again. That was fine. But your cotton-picking ability is all your own, Tom Stevens."

Then he turned to the crowd around them and called out, "Come up here, Jimmy and Patricia! It's you who made it possible for Tom Stevens to compete. You should present him with the prize."

The two children came forward delightedly. In another minute, Patricia held in her hand the precious red ribbon of honor with the words, *First Prize,* printed on it in white letters. She stepped over to Tom and pinned it on his shirt. Then Jimmy handed him an envelope containing the money prize of twenty-five dollars.

Tom bowed to him and Patricia, to Mr. Byrnes and the committee, to Mr. and Mrs. Archer and then to all the assembled crowd. "Thank you, thank you," he said again and again.

Then the band struck up a rousing gay tune, and the people all went to their family groups to have their picnic lunches in the cool grove along the creek.

Orange Blossom Time

FLORIDA

IT was dawn at the Forbes orange grove in Florida. From the veranda of their home, Peter, Kay, and Dave watched a car as it went down the palm-lined driveway and through the gates that separated the garden from the citrus grove. "Good-by, Mother!" they called. "Good-by, Dad!"

When the car had disappeared into the morning mists on its way to the station, the children sat down on the top step. Their black-and-white setter, Dollar, stretched out beside them and rested his head in Dave's lap.

"Why are Mother and Dad making their trip to New York now?" asked Dave, who was nine and liked to ask questions. "Dad always likes to be here to see the crop picked, and it's almost ready, isn't it?"

"Yes," replied Peter, who was thirteen and knew all about the routine on the orange grove. "But the packing-house men won't get around to picking our crop for a few weeks. They're working on some big 5,000-acre groves that belong to a company."

"But why did Dad have to leave Florida when we've just staked off that ten acres for our new grove?" persisted Dave.

Patiently his brother answered, "The nurseryman said he wouldn't be able to bring his trucks out here to set out the young trees until the end of the month. Dad and Mother expect to get home by then. Anyway, Dave, this trip is unexpected. Dad just found out that he would have to make a business trip to New York sometime in February."

"So, you see," said Kay, "this was really just the right time for them to go. But we won't feel too lonesome without them because we have Uncle Cribbs with us."

"He isn't any fun. He has rheumatism," Dave reminded her.

"I know." She frowned a little. During her parents' absence, Uncle Cribbs was to be her special care. Her uncle, whose home was in Chicago, had been ill and was still in a wheel chair. He had come to Florida to escape the severe winter weather of the North.

By now, the mists were lifting, and the orange trees could be seen with their waxy green leaves glistening in the sunshine. The light fell upon the blooms, which were clustered like pearls beside the golden fruit.

Kay went into the house, and her brothers went out to the barn to feed their saddle horses. When they had finished, they were surprised to hear the sound of trucks roaring up the road that led to the pump-house by the lake. The trucks stopped before the row of cabins occupied by the families who worked on the Forbes grove.

"Hello, Peter! Hello, Dave!" called a man, jumping from the first truck as the boys came up.

They recognized him as the owner of the nursery that had been given the order to plant the new grove at the end of the month.

"Well," he said, beaming at the Forbes boys, "here we are. That other job I'd expected to be on until the end of the month has folded up, so I thought I'd surprise your father by planting his grove today. Run and tell him we're here." He called to the men in one of the other trucks, "Jump out and let's get started!"

Peter and Dave looked at each other in bewilderment.

"But Dad has left for New York," said Peter.

Now it was the nurseryman's turn to look bewildered. "Gone to New York?"

A dozen workers had jumped out of the trucks. Some of them unloaded tools. Others lifted out a pump and set it at the edge of the lake. In a jiffy, water began pouring through a hose into the barrels on one of the trucks, while from a covered truck another crew started removing the leafless stalks that were the pruned, budded young trees with their long tap roots. Peter and his brother knew that these trees would have to be put into the ground at once.

"Too bad your father isn't on hand," shrugged the nurseryman. "I know he wanted to watch the planting. Where's your caretaker?"

"Joe's driving Mother and Dad to the train," Dave answered.

"I need two workers at once," said the nurseryman. "I'm short of help today. Where are your father's other men?" He glanced over at the deserted cabins.

Peter explained, "They're working in the grove. Can't Dave and I help you? We'd have to miss school, but this is an emergency." He turned to his brother. "What d'you say, Dave?"

"I say we help," was the younger boy's quick decision. "You start. I'll go and tell Kay the big excitement." Like a flash, he was off.

In the meantime, Kay was pushing Uncle Cribbs into the sunny garden. He enjoyed the sight of butterflies in February, and the music of mockingbirds singing from a magnolia tree. About him were bright flowers—scarlet hibiscus, blue plumbago, yellow jasmine, and roses. Over the garden's edge were great oaks, from which long strands of gray Spanish moss swung in the breeze. Ahead and far beyond, he saw the lakes and woods and groves of the "ridge country" stretching toward the horizon. Uncle Cribbs was admiring all this tropical beauty when Dave raced up with the news that the new grove was to be planted.

"Oh," Kay gasped. "You mean—they're actually putting in the trees, and Dad not here?"

"Yes. And Peter and I aren't going to school today. We've got to help. It's an emergency. The trees will die if they're not put in right away. You know that."

"Well!" said Kay. "Dad will certainly be surprised when he hears what's happened."

Just then Lillie Mae, the cook, called from the side

door, "The packing house telephoned! They just said to tell Mr. Forbes that they'd begun picking fruit on his place today, that they were out on the north forty acres."

Kay moaned. "Oh, Dad had planned to be here when they came for the first picking. It seems that everything that wasn't expected has happened!"

Then she laughed. "This morning I thought things were going to be dull with Dad and Mother away," she confided to her uncle, "but we're having a heap of excitement, aren't we?"

In spite of his rheumatism, Uncle Cribbs chuckled.

"You tell Lillie Mae to wheel me over to see the planting," he said to Kay. "After lunch I want to go and watch the picking."

Peter was laying trees beside stakes along the row that edged the lawn, when he came upon Uncle Cribbs later that morning in his wheel chair. His uncle was alone, except for Dollar, who was standing guard beside the chair.

"I'm here to watch the planting," announced Uncle Cribbs. "How much ground are you going to plant, boy?"

"Ten acres," Peter told him. "And there'll be sixty-seven trees to the acre. It'll be finished today."

Uncle Cribbs whistled. "That's hard to believe."

"Oh, the job's easier than it may look to you," replied his nephew, setting a young tree down beside a stake near the chair. "The ground has already been prepared, and the rows marked off, and stakes driven into holes made for the trees. See this long tap root?" Uncle Cribbs leaned forward intently and nodded. "It will be dropped into the hole marked by the stake. The crew that follows us will do that. Well, I've got to move on!"

The planting crew was close upon Peter's heels. Uncle Cribbs watched them carefully. A stake was withdrawn, and the long tap root of the small leafless tree was dropped into its hole. The fibre roots hung naturally into a place the planter prepared on each side of the stake hole, and the dirt was sifted and "watered" about those two sets of roots. The crown roots were left even with the earth. A cupped mound of dirt, to hold the water, was shaped about the tree.

Immediately came the watering crew who brought buckets of water carried from barrels on one of the trucks. The workers who followed took great pains to "firm" the earth about each tree, and to "bank" it for the winter by leaving soil high about it to keep out the cold and retain the moisture.

The work on the row edging the lawn was finished when Lillie Mae came to wheel Uncle Cribbs back to the house for lunch.

During the meal, while the boys and their uncle were talking over the big excitement of the day, Peter tuned in on the radio in the dining room. He was just in time to catch the weather report. The forecast was for temperatures that would be dangerous for citrus fruit within forty-eight hours!

"I hope that doesn't mean a freeze here!" Peter exclaimed. "With Dad away, that would be some job for us."

"A freeze?" His uncle frowned. "I thought I came here to get away from a freeze."

Peter assured him quickly. "Oh, we probably won't have one. We haven't had a freeze here for several years. We might have a frost, but that wouldn't harm the crop, nor the trees, either."

With all this talk about a freeze or a frost, Uncle Cribbs was getting a bit fidgety. To the boys' surprise, hc said, "Your Dad may be away, but don't forget that I'm here. I expect to be told what to do to protect the grove in case of a freeze."

"But your rheumatism—" began Dave.

"Rheumatism?" his uncle almost shouted. "Your Florida sunshine has made me feel spry as a cricket. I'm not going to get into that wheel chair after today. If a freeze hits us, I'll help save the oranges and the trees."

That afternoon, Joe pushed Uncle Cribbs into the bearing part of the grove to watch the pickers gather the golden fruit. He stayed there all afternoon until Kay returned from school.

"Oh, so, here you are!" she called when she found

him. "I really think you look better today, Uncle Cribbs."

"I feel better, too," he declared. "What are those metal boxes for?" He pointed to containers about thirty inches high that were placed by every other tree, in alternating rows.

"They're smudge cans," replied Kay. "We light them to make a 'smudge' in case of a freeze."

"We have 6,000 trees here," said Joe solemnly. "If a freeze should come, we would have to fire up the grove to save the oranges. We have ninety acres of fruit—a fine crop. We keep the grove ready to be fired, although we haven't had a freeze in several years. In a part of the grove we just burn pine wood between the rows. You've noticed that we have lots of it stacked throughout the grove?"

"Yes, I have," said Uncle Cribbs. "But what about the new grove, if a freeze comes?"

"Why, don't you remember that the planters 'banked' those young trees?" asked Kay.

"There are some rows of trees near the lake that have no protection," put in Joe. "If by tomorrow noon, the cold spell is still on its way, I'll get out those old tires and put them between the rows. We can make a good smudge by burning crude oil in them."

Never having seen oranges harvested before, Uncle Cribbs enjoyed watching the fifteen pickers at work. Standing on their ladders, they swiftly clipped the golden

balls and dropped them into their sacks. Each man had to make two trips down his ladder with his sack full of fruit before he could fill one field box. For a long while Uncle Cribbs watched the small farm tractors, pulling two-wheel trailers, passing between the rows of trees, depositing empty boxes, and picking up the filled ones. Then Joe returned to push him to the house.

"What about packing?" Uncle Cribbs asked Kay. "Don't you orange growers pack your own fruit?"

"No, we don't bother about that," she told him. "The packing house does it better and cheaper. It has machinery, too, for cleaning and waxing the oranges, and for culling out the out-sized fruit for the canneries."

The next day, while the children were in school, their uncle found that he could walk about the place easily without suffering from rheumatism. At noon, he listened to the weather forecast and heard the bad news. Temperatures dangerously low for citrus groves were predicted for the following morning in the Polk County area. The news made him aware of the fact that the air was already cooler than it had been.

He told the children about the forecast when they came home. At once, they rushed out to find Joe and consult with him about getting help for the "firing" of the grove if it should become necessary. They could not remember when Joe had looked so serious.

Joe and Dave took the old tires out to the trees near the lake and filled them with crude oil. Peter went out and spoke to the pickers, and they all promised to return that night and bring others to help, too. A chill had been settling over the grove, and a northwest wind was blowing. The thermometer on the barn registered 50 degrees when the boys were feeding their horses at sunset.

"They're having a blizzard in Chicago," reported Uncle Cribbs as he turned off the radio just before supper. "I'm glad I'm not there."

At eight o'clock, Dave looked at the thermometer outside of the dining-room window and reported a temperature of 44.

That evening, when the great campfire was built on the grass back of the house, twenty-seven helpers were there, in addition to the men who lived on the place. All were eager to help. Many of them, like the Forbes children, having been born and reared in the state, knew the dangers of a real freeze and the ruin it could bring to a citrus grove.

The intense heat of the fire was welcome, for by eleven o'clock the temperature had dropped to 38 degrees, and the wind was blowing harder.

The watchers sat on benches about the fire, singing, joking, telling ghost stories, and peeling oranges with their pocket knives. Uncle Cribbs was among them.

Joe kept the fire roaring, and at intervals sent men to read thermometers at various locations throughout the grove. It was Peter's job to keep a constant check on the temperature and to give the order to the men to begin "firing" as soon as it dropped to 30 degrees.

"Of course," Kay explained to Uncle Cribbs, "28 degrees is the really dangerous low, and even at 26 the oranges would be safe for an hour or two without freezing."

It became colder and colder. Lillie Mae brought out a blanket and tucked it about Uncle Cribbs' shoulders. By midnight, the temperature had dropped to 36 degrees. Kay and Dave helped Lillie Mae bring out coffee and doughnuts and sandwiches for the hungry men.

The wind kept up, and the temperature kept dropping.

It was three o'clock in the morning when it dropped to 30 degrees. Peter gave the order: *"Fire the grove!"*

Everybody jumped into action. Each worker knew in advance what his own task would be to help save the fruit and blossoms on Mr. Forbes' 6,000 trees. The crews who were to work near-by were quick to light their torches and begin.

Kay and Dave and Uncle Cribbs helped in the nearest rows where stacks of pine wood and the smudge cans had to be lighted. Crews that were to go to the more distant trees climbed into trucks and rumbled off into the darkness. Soon the smell of burning pine filled the air as stacks of wood and smudge cans sent out their smoke, and the strong odor of oil came drifting through the trees.

Peter and Joe went to check on the work of the crews. "Hey, this stack of wood isn't burning!" they would call out. Or, "Wait until I relight this smudge can—it's gone out!"

By five o'clock in the morning the temperature had

dropped to 28 degrees, where it stayed for nearly an hour. The men returned to the campfire to await further developments. Would all of this combined heat and smoke save the fruit and blossoms?

At last, at sunrise, the temperature was up to 30 degrees. It was rising faster now. To everyone's joy, the wind began shifting so that it came from the north. Then it shifted gradually to the east. This meant that before the day was over the wind would be coming from the southeast, bringing warm air from the ocean, and ending the danger of a freeze.

The battle against the freeze was over! The workers were happy as they trooped into the great Forbes kitchen for breakfast. From Lillie Mae's tired hands they received plates filled with steaming grits and eggs. Upon the tables were muffins, butter, coffee, and cream.

The Forbes children entered the kitchen with Uncle Cribbs. Their faces were smudged, their eyes smarted, and their backs ached.

"School today?" their uncle asked in fun.

"School?" Lillie Mae handed them steaming plates and put glasses of hot milk on a table for them. "Well, I guess not! It's bed for these children—and you, too, Mr. Cribbs."

Choosing Day

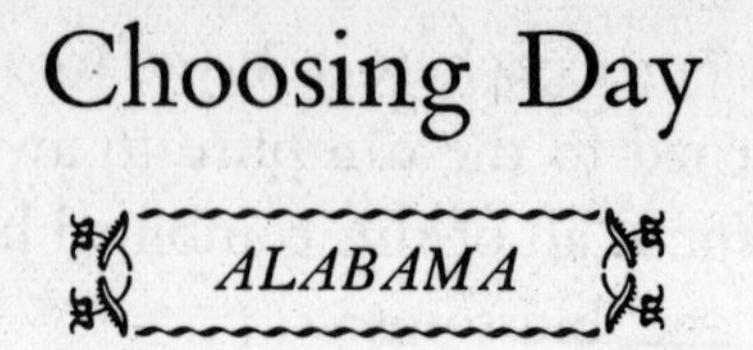

"ALABAM', here I am . . . Alabam', here I am . . ." purred the motor of the blue-and-silver bus. Ellen from far Vermont was traveling southward through Alabama where she was going to spend the winter. Her mother had come with her as far as Birmingham, but Ellen was making the rest of the trip alone.

Seated at the window, she looked out hour after hour across yellow rivers and at spreading fields still white-flecked with the last of the cotton. She looked into dim forests where, hanging from the trees, was the queer trailing Spanish moss—enough of it to make beards for all the dwarfs in fairyland, she decided.

And at last—yes! at last the big bus pulled up at the station. There was tall Uncle John Mitchell, and plump Aunt Hallie Mitchell, and an automobile full of lively Mitchell cousins, all waiting to take Ellen to Pinelands Plantation.

"Flowers here! And think of it—I left home in the middle of an early snowstorm!" cried Ellen later as they arrived at the plantation, and she saw red roses and gay beds of marigold and bushes bright with lovely yellow flowers.

Very different, too, from her compact northern home was the rambling, white-columned Pinelands house with its great porches on all four sides. Behind the large house were several other buildings solid and strong and a hundred years old, like the plantation house itself. There was a brick-walled dairy house with a well, a dove cote, and a squared-log smokehouse. There were houses for the servants and a barn with a large bell in its tower that called men to and from the fields.

Oh, it was going to be fun here! Next-door neighbors were the Wiltons of Mile-Square-Farm. The lawns of these two plantation homes came together in one spreading green level, with never a sign of a fence between. Ellen soon found that her cousins and the Wiltons all worked and played together so much that they were almost like one big family.

To Ellen from far Vermont, this promised to be a happy winter, except—well, there *was* a something that Ellen knew she was going to miss terribly. Why, winter wouldn't really seem like winter without it! But, being polite, she firmly decided that she must say nothing about it.

Anyway, her cousins and the Wiltons thought of so many interesting things to do that Ellen hardly had time for any homesick thoughts. On Saturdays, they went on hikes through the woods to the Indian Mound. It was a large, curious, flat-topped cone of earth. Jim told her about the ancient Spanish cannon that had been dredged out of the Alabama River just around the bend from the Mound.

"That shows," said her cousin proudly, "that DeSoto, or some one of those famous old Spanish explorers who were the first white men to set foot in what is now Alabama, must have passed right near this very spot!"

But in spite of hikes, and games, and fun, and in spite of the cakes that Maum Dilsey stirred up in the kitchen, Ellen did have a feeling of homesickness for that certain "something" that made her northern winters so happy.

On the last afternoon in November, as they all sat out on the wide front porch eating ginger cup-cakes, she

found herself asking, "Without any snow to fall, or any ice to melt away, how do you ever know when winter comes and goes or when spring begins? And how can you tell when summer ends and autumn begins? I should think you'd get all mixed up."

Neena munched her cake thoughtfully as they gazed off beyond the high white columns of the house. "Oh, that's easy," she replied. "It's spring when the first wood violets pop up, purple and velvety from beneath the pine straw—"

"Summer means peaches and watermelons and Fourth o' July!" chanted Honey and Bub. And Honey added, "And putting long white hairs from Old Gray Nag's tail in the rain barrel to see if they'll turn into snakes—only they never do."

Everybody laughed. The sweetness of the red roses came drifting toward the children.

Jim continued, "It's autumn when the crunchy, sweet pecan nuts fall—and walnuts, and hickory, and chestnuts, and scalybarks, and chinquapins (ching'ka pins)."

"What are *scalybarks* and *chinquapins?"* asked Ellen.

Neena explained that scalybarks were thin-shelled nuts rather like hickory and easy to crack. "We often use them to make heads for small homemade dolls," she added. "And chinquapins are rather like chestnuts. Um-m! are they good! We prick the shells with a pin and roast the nuts on a shovel over glowing coals."

"And winter," concluded little Patsy, "is when we gather all the green tomatoes in the garden and set them on the high shelf in the pantry to ripen slowly. And when we hope the roses will be blooming for Christmas. And when we have Choosing Day and Game Day."

"Choosing Day and Game Day?" Ellen asked.

"Hurrah!" shouted red-headed Sue, tossing up her hands. "Didn't we tell you that tomorrow's Game Day, the first day of December? That means today is Choosing Day. So, let's get down to business!"

"Yes, yes!" they all agreed, including Ellen, although she had no idea what they were talking about.

Now they all raced for the old playroom up on the third floor of the Mitchell home. Breathlessly, Sue explained that the Mitchells and the Wiltons called the first day of December, Game Day, when they always had a picnic on Pine-Top Knob and played games. The day before they called Choosing Day, when each child chose one game or toy, as his specialty for the picnic fun.

As they ran through the hall, a spicy fragrance came out of the kitchen, and from the doorway Mrs. Mitchell waved a big spoon. "We're making a start on tomorrow's lunch!" she called after the children. "But I was beginning to think you'd all grown too big for Choosing Day, or had forgotten it."

"Oh, no!"

"We have some extra plans this year!"

"On to the attic!"

Their happy voices drifted back above the clatter of racing feet on the stairs. Mrs. Mitchell and Maum Dilsey laughed together in the kitchen.

In the old playroom, were chests and trunks and boxes.

"A boat for mine," stated Jim, lifting the top of a wooden chest and taking out a toy boat with all sails set. "Who'll choose another so we can race 'em tomorrow on the pond?"

"A boat for me—" "and me," chorused the two little boys who always followed Jim's lead.

Patsy chose a tiny tea set and planned to have a tea-party on Pine-Top Knob. Honey found a ball and jacks. Neena chose some beanbags for a game of beanbag tag. Sue's choice was a game of ring-toss.

Then Neena suddenly exclaimed, looking at the others with flashing eyes, "Aren't we the impolite ones! Here, Ellen's company and ought to have first choice of all. Do take your pick, Ellen, and please excuse us. We were very rude."

"Take mine!" they all invited at once.

Ellen looked at the boats and at Neena's beanbags and then at the other things which were held out to her.

"There are still lots of things in the old trunk," suggested Jim.

"Just choose the game you like best," urged little Patsy, "and we'll play it tomorrow, first thing."

"I choose—" began Ellen. She closed her eyes. "I choose to go sledding." Then she opened her eyes. She hadn't meant to say that at all. The words had just popped out before she could stop them. That was her secret wish—the longing to go sledding down a snowy hill. But, of course, in this sunny land of the South, there were no sleds because there was no snowy hill.

The Wilton children looked at the Mitchells, and the Mitchell children looked at the Wiltons. A startled look spread over their faces.

"I know something—" began little Patsy. But Jim and Sue began to talk very loud and fast about the time they would start in the morning—"early so as to make the most of the day."

Ellen stood there forlornly in the middle of the attic. How rude she felt, asking for something that just couldn't be had. "No, no," she stammered out. "I mean, I choose—checkers." This was the first game she could think of.

Laughing and talking, they all trooped back down the stairs and out to the kitchen. They fell to work with a will, whipping up egg whites for spice-cake frosting, and picking out nut meats for the pecan fudge for the picnic. After a mysterious whispering with Neena, however, Sue and Jim slipped away and were seen no more until suppertime.

Game Day came in bright and sunny. Directly after breakfast, the Mitchells and the Wiltons gathered and soon were off for the picnic grounds. Jim was already on the way, driving the wagon in which were Mrs. Mitchell, Maum Dilsey, and her big pot for the cocoa-making, the well-packed lunch baskets, and a mound of lumpy objects well covered by an old blanket robe.

The rest went on foot, tramping across a corner of the cotton field, through the sugar-cane patch with its next year's seed-cane banked under great earthen ridges. Then on they went through the nut grove, beyond the pasture, and up a steep hill.

"This is Pine-Top Knob," panted Patsy who was walking beside Ellen. "We're 'most to the picnic grounds—oh, there's a nice flat stone for my tea-party table." She skipped off to one side, where in a shallow dip in the hillside, ferns grew around a large rock.

"The pond for sailing the boats is on the other side of the Knob!" Jim called back to Ellen, as he and the other boys sprinted ahead.

Everybody was excited over Game Day! As she climbed to the summit of Pine-Top Knob, Ellen wished she felt a little more excited, too. But she simply couldn't when there wasn't even a chance for her favorite winter sport of sledding!

Then, after the last upward scramble, there she stood on the crest of the hill. But what were those things she saw now in front of her? Not sleds! Yes—they were actually *sleds!* Not handsome, shiny, red-and-blue, store-bought sleds, to be sure—but squatty, stubbly, homemade ones with barrel-staves for runners and with little bells tied on the front.

Ellen dropped to her knees beside one of them, her eyes shining.

"Oh—sleds!" she exclaimed, and shook the little bells to hear them jingle. "I didn't know you had sleds, 'way down here in Alabama. But you have no ice or snow to coast on—"

Jim interrupted. "Our snow's *brown snow,"* he laughed, kicking up a flurry of the pine straw that covered Pine-Top Knob in a thick, slippery carpet.

"Hi . . . yi!" shouted the little boys. "We'll show you how fine our brown snow is to coast on!" Each grabbed up a little sled, plopped down on it, and away they went down the slope as fast as ever a sled flew down a Vermont hill covered with snow.

Right behind, came Jim and Ellen on another pair of sleds.

Oh, Ellen thought it was glorious! Down, down, down. Over the glossy brown pine needles, the sleds flew like winged things.

Back up the hill came the whole troop, dragging their sleds. Then down again they coasted. Up and down they went until their appetites were so big it was a good thing the lunch baskets were packed to the bursting point.

Um-m-yum! How good Maum Dilsey's great hubbly-bubbly pot of cocoa did smell, standing there over the fire which Jim had laid the day before, ready for lighting on Game Day.

Now the youngsters had to try coasting, three at a time, on the longest sled, a solid plank window-shutter, with runners made from the staves of a sugar hogshead.

"Sleds and a sliding hill—but how did you ever get all this ready and keep it a secret?" asked Ellen.

"Oh, we do this kind of sliding all year around," Sue told her. "But we figured that you might be homesick for snow slides, so we decided this year to save the sliding as a surprise for you on Game Day."

"Yesterday," continued Neena, "when you said 'I choose to go sledding,' we all got so flustered that we nearly gave the secret away."

Ellen's eyes were twinkly with happiness. "You did keep the secret, and you did surprise me. Oh, I must have one more ride before lunch—" And as Ellen went skimming like the wind down the steep, brown hillside, she shouted back to them, "Who'd have thought I'd be sledding 'way down south in Alabam'? Three cheers for brown snow!"

The Candlelight Ball

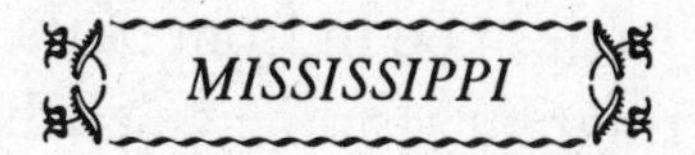

"HURRAH for Green Oaks!" sang Betsy as the taxi in which she was riding drove through the familiar gates of her grandfather's Mississippi plantation near Natchez.

"We'll be there soon," said her Cousin Arch who was riding in the front seat with the driver.

Now they were driving along a shady sunken road where rose vines trailed their pink-and-white blossoms over the sides. Tulip trees, sycamores, and sweet-gum trees grew on either edge of the road. Then the road began to rise, and the car climbed into the glare of the late morning sun. Some distance beyond, a broad expanse of water could be seen.

"Old Man River!" sang out Arch. "We're almost there now."

There lay the Mississippi with silvery beeches and willows growing along its banks. The taxi was now following a driveway bordered with boxwood. Soon it stopped in front of the ancient house, Green Oaks, which had been standing there since Spanish colonial times.

Betsy and Arch had been invited to their grandfather's home for the annual Pilgrimage. For a month during the Pilgrimage the lovely old houses in and near Natchez were open to visitors. People came from many parts of the country to see these old Natchez homes.

As Betsy and Arch stood in front of the old house, they could smell the fragrant jasmine vine which twined over the white columns of the veranda. The door was opened by their grandfather. Tall, straight, and gray-haired, he called out, "Welcome to Green Oaks!"

"Welcome, indeed, Betsy and Archie!" echoed a dainty little white-haired lady who stood behind their grandfather. She was Great-Greataunt Mary and was very old.

A few moments later they stepped into the hallway of the house. In the drawing room beyond, gilt-framed mirrors reflected the chandeliers with their twinkling crystal prisms. That night at the Candlelight Ball, these prisms would shed the soft glow of many candles.

Now footsteps clattered on the spiral staircase as

Cousin Sinclair, a boy of ten, came running down, shouting, "Hello, Cousins!"

"How nice to have you here again," Aunt Letitia greeted them.

"We're so glad to be here, Aunt Letitia!" exclaimed Arch.

Betsy laughed and gave her aunt a hug. "We're so excited, we want to look around right away."

In the dining room they stood before the long rosewood table. In the center of the table was a bowl of yellow roses.

Sinclair pointed out the shining silver goblets on the sideboard. "I polished 'em," he boasted.

"Yes, this is one time of the year when Sinclair really does some chores," observed Grandfather with twinkling eyes. "You know, these are the same goblets that Mammy Dilcey's mother hid one day during the Civil War."

"We never did know what became of the silver pitcher that matched them," Great-Greataunt Mary said with a little sigh.

Betsy and Arch had heard the story of the goblets many times before, but they listened eagerly just the same.

"Leah, our cook, carried them outdoors in an apron filled with turnip greens," continued their grandfather, just as though he had never before told the story. "The yard was full of Yankee soldiers but, of course, they thought she was merely dumping out some vegetable tops. That night she wrapped the goblets in a sack and lowered them into the dried-up cistern where they stayed until her mistress came home after the war."

"They sure did," affirmed Mammy Dilcey from the doorway. There she stood in her plaid dress and large white apron with a white kerchief around her head. She beamed at the young visitors. "Seems like the good old times when your daddies were boys here together rampin' over the plantation."

"It's nice to see you, Mammy," said Betsy, and Arch added, "It's good old times to me when I can eat some of your fine cooking."

Mammy Dilcey chuckled, "Well, I reckon in a little while I'm going to serve lunch out in the patio under the big oak."

"Now do come into the library," Great-Greataunt Mary invited mysteriously.

In the book-lined library with the black marble fireplace, they gathered before a portrait of a lovely young girl wearing a white satin frock embroidered with seed pearls around the low-cut shoulders.

"Tonight, Betsy, I want your hair put up into curls just like mine in my portrait here," said Great-Greataunt Mary. "And I want you to wear my old dress to the Candlelight Ball."

"Oh!" exclaimed Betsy. "Will you let me wear it, really?"

The old lady smiled. "Yes, honey. I've been looking forward to having you wear it tonight at the ball. You're just the age I was when I last wore it. That was—oh, do let me see—more than eighty years ago."

"And here it is!" announced Aunt Letitia, coming into the library, and holding the white satin dress up to Betsy. "It's a trifle short, but we can easily drop the hem."

"Say, you'll look swell," Arch remarked proudly, and his Cousin Sinclair agreed.

Fondly, Betsy touched the smooth satin. She knew the dress had come from Paris long, long ago. "You dear," she murmured, putting her arms around the little old lady.

"Julina is waiting upstairs in your room," said Aunt Letitia. "She wants you to try the dress on, and then she will press it for you. And lunch will soon be ready." She looked at the two boys.

"Good!" they shouted.

A little while later they all gathered in the patio where the table was set in the shade of the great oak tree. Beyond the rose garden, the lawn sloped away to the river shimmering in the sunlight. They sipped iced tea with mint leaves and helped themselves to salad and sliced turkey. For dessert they had syllabub, sweetened cream beaten to a stiff froth and flavored with wine, and crispy southern rolled wafers.

"This syllabub and these wafers were made from an old family recipe," Aunt Letitia told her niece and nephew.

"I could eat wafers by the dozen," said Arch.

"Well," observed his grandfather, "you haven't far to go, young man. I believe you've had nine already," he added while everybody laughed.

Immediately after lunch, Betsy jumped up. "I know it isn't polite to go running away from the table," she told Aunt Letitia, "but Arch and Sinclair and I have to attend to something right away. It's more important than anything that's ever happened here at Green Oaks since—since Mammy Dilcey's mother hid the silver goblets during the Civil War and—"

"Say, what are you talking about?" demanded Arch.

"That's what I want to know," added Sinclair.

"You'll see," replied Betsy mysteriously as they followed her from the patio.

"Be sure you come back in plenty of time to get into your costumes!" Grandfather called after them.

"We will!" they promised.

As Betsy led the way around the house, she told her cousins, "It's going to make this Pilgrimage the most exciting one Great-Greataunt Mary has ever seen."

"What can all the excitement be?" murmured Great-Greataunt Mary as she sipped her iced tea.

That evening at candlelighting hour, the family and a gathering of friends—all in old-fashioned costumes—met in the large, double drawing room of Green Oaks. Sofas and chairs were ranged against the walls for the guests, and four hundred slender white candles were glowing in the chandeliers and candelabra. The soft candlelight was reflected in the mirrors and on the gleaming dance floor.

The scent of locust blossoms and the song of a bird drifted in through the open French windows.

"Oh, how lovely," breathed Betsy.

"Shelley, our mockingbird, is singing in the garden," Sinclair told her. "He sings there every evening."

Silently they stood listening to the song, rising and falling like sparkling water in a fountain. Then they heard the crunching of tires on the driveway.

"Here come the first of the guests!" said Aunt Letitia excitedly. "Let's stand in our places to greet them. Boys, you look too handsome for words in your gray Confederate uniforms."

As the different groups of guests arrived, Mammy Dilcey with shining smiles hung up their wraps in the back hall. The two boys, and Betsy in the Paris gown with her hair put up in curls, showed them through the library and the other rooms. There was a continuous hum of talk as more and more people arrived and strolled about, enjoying the beauty of Green Oaks.

At last, from the small musicians' balcony at the far end of the back drawing room came the sounds of the orchestra tuning up.

"Time for the Grand March!" Sinclair whispered to Betsy.

The family and their friends now went upstairs. As the violin, cello, flute, and harp began to play *General Beauregard's March,* they started down the graceful spiral staircase.

Grandfather, in his Confederate colonel's gold-buttoned gray uniform, escorted Great-Greataunt Mary. She was dressed in a lavender brocade and wore a lace cap on her silver curls. Next, in regimentals, came the

Governor of Mississippi, and Aunt Letitia lovely in an old blue hoop-skirted gown. Sinclair followed with Betsy in Great-Greataunt Mary's pearl-embroidered satin dress. Arch was the escort of a neighbor's daughter wearing a billowy pink gown with ruffles. The others followed, gay in their colorful costumes.

At the foot of the stairs, the guests formed into a double line for the Grand March while Grandfather led Great-Greataunt Mary to a chair in the library. Across the hall, through the drawing room and library—then back across the hall again into the dining room in a great circle. Around and around they marched while Great-Greataunt Mary sat in the library and smiled at them as they passed.

Then the orchestra played an old waltz, and as everybody danced to it, they seemed to be whirled back through time to other nights long ago when other candles glowed in the same crystal prisms and other waltz music floated through the same rooms at Green Oaks.

Later in the evening the children joined Great-Greataunt Mary. They found her standing below her portrait. She was talking to the Governor.

"Tell us about your portrait," begged Betsy who always loved to hear Great-Greataunt Mary tell the story.

The little old lady looked into the children's eager faces. "Why, you've heard it so many times," she said.

"I know," replied Betsy, "but we want to hear it

again—especially at the Candlelight Ball this year." Her cousins caught the mysterious tone in her voice, but Great-Greataunt Mary did not seem to notice.

"Do tell us, Aunt Mary!" Arch begged, nudging Sinclair in the ribs.

"Yes, do tell us again!" urged his cousin.

"Well, I was eleven years old," began Great-Greataunt Mary in her sweet quiet way as she sat down in a chair. She did not see that Grandfather had signaled the orchestra to stop playing and that the guests were silently gathering there in the library. "Here in this very room, Mother was sitting there by the hearth, reading *David Copperfield* to me. I was over there by the window, working on my embroidery. Above the mantel, hung my portrait—as it is hanging now.

"All of a sudden, Leah, our cook, came rushing into the room. 'Mis' Isabelle!' she cried to Mother. 'Cicero rode up, a-gallopin' from the lower plantation! He says the river is crawlin' with Yankee gunboats! What'll we do?'

" 'Have Chloe get out our traveling clothes,' said Mother.

"Mother and I took down my portrait from the wall. Soon the coach came dashing up to the front door. The coachman cracked his whip, and the high-stepping black horses drove Mother and Chloe and me away under the magnolia branches. It seemed to me the trees on the plantation with their trailing Spanish moss were weeping for us because we must leave our beloved Green Oaks."

At this point in the story, Betsy slipped quietly out of the room.

"We had the portrait with us," continued Great-Greataunt Mary, "and a trunk in the 'boot' of the carriage with all the silver which Leah had not had time to hide."

As Aunt Mary paused in her story, one of the guests asked, "Where did you go?"

"To our uncle's plantation in northern Mississippi," answered Great-Greataunt Mary. "When we came back after the war, Leah was gone and as Mother and I never knew all the places where she had hidden our silver, many things were lost. I especially regret the silver pitcher that belonged with the goblets—the ones on the sideboard in the dining room."

These words seemed to be an anticipated signal. For Arch and Sinclair immediately led Great-Greataunt Mary out to the hall where Betsy was waiting on the staircase.

Everyone now gathered there in the hall—the Governor and Grandfather, Aunt Letitia and all of the guests. Then Mammy Dilcey appeared and stood on the stairs beside Betsy.

"The silver pitcher!" everybody exclaimed. *"The old silver pitcher!"*

Yes, there stood Mammy with the lovely pitcher and the goblets on a silver tray!

As soon as the murmur of voices had subsided, Betsy spoke. Her eyes were shining with the excitement of it all.

"Today when we let down the hem of Great-Great-aunt Mary's dress so that it would be the proper length for me to wear tonight, a scrap of paper came fluttering out. It was a note, written long ago, and signed by Leah! Leah was the family cook who had buried some of the family silver during the Civil War."

Now Betsy held up a piece of paper and read the almost faded words: " 'Small trunk—summerhouse—near brick wall—Leah.'

"My cousins and I dug up the little trunk this afternoon," Betsy continued, thrilled to be telling the story, "and in it we found the pitcher and the tray to match!"

"Then I boiled 'em in soda water in a tin tub," announced Arch, taking his place beside Betsy. "I put in some metal strips—and the tarnish came right off."

Sinclair added, "And I polished them."

Great-Greataunt Mary reached up and lovingly touched the gleaming silver design of vine and grapes on the old pitcher.

"Leah, dear old Leah," she said softly as though talking to somebody the others could not see. "This is one of the lovely nights of my life."

Of course, they must all go out into the moonlight under the locust trees, and down the walk by the camellia hedge to the summerhouse to see where the little trunk had been hidden that time so long ago. Then they came strolling back to the patio. The stars twinkled through the branches of the great oak. Music floated out through the night, and again the mockingbird was singing in the garden.

"There will be other Candlelight Balls here at Green Oaks," said Betsy as she went in to dance with her Cousin Sinclair. "But there never will be—oh, there never can be—another like the one this year!"

Rising Waters

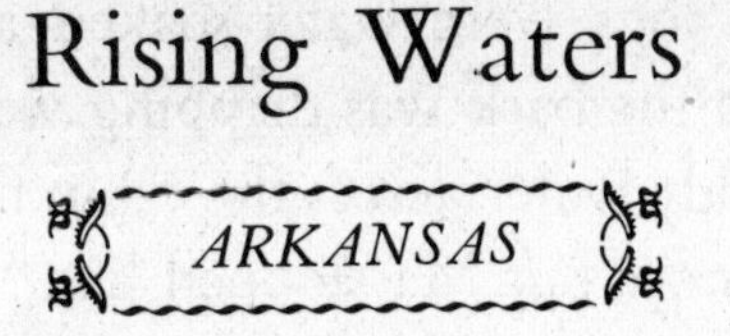

ALL night long the wind had been blowing about the cabin. It whistled through the chinks, laying its thin cool fingers against the walls as though trying to pry out the mud and plaster. Sometimes a special gust would wrap its arms about the little log house as though to shake it into submission.

Up under the eaves in the loft where she slept, Lucy Mae could feel the gusts playing over her face, and she cuddled down under the homemade coverlet, thankful for its comfort.

"There'll be rain before daybreak," Pa had said and Lucy Mae could feel it coming closer and closer with every onslaught of the wind. It seemed as if there was rain everywhere this year. Here it was only January, and the rain was a-raining and a-raining like Old Noah's flood coming back. It wasn't in nature to have so much water falling around everywhere.

The storm broke with the cold dawn, and Pa coming in from the woodpile brought all the logs he could carry and went back for more. "We'd better put them under cover," he said. "It looks as if all Arkansas is going to have a flood, and we'd better keep the wood dry."

Already the logs were water-soaked and the rough, brown moss on the bark was dripping wet, sending tiny rivulets of muddy water across the cabin floor. Lucy Mae hurried for a mop, but Ma stopped her.

"There'll be more than that before your Pa gets through," she said. "You'd better wait and mop it all at once. Move the reed-bottomed chair and the rocking chair and make room by the hearth for most of the wood. The kindling can go back in the storeroom."

It was back-breaking work for Pa, tugging at the big logs, gathering the kindling in the big cotton basket and piling the chips in the bushel basket. Higher and higher rose the pile of steaming logs. The trickling water sizzled on the worn stones of the hearth and sent little bursts of steam through the cabin.

"It's good wood, if it is a little wet," Pa said, as he dumped the last log on the hearth and set the chips back in the chimney corner. He ate breakfast hungrily, spearing the bacon from the three-legged skillet set in the ashes, and pouring the thin pork gravy on his corn bread.

"Keep the child in," he said to his wife, pausing between mouthfuls. "It's no day for her to go to school. She might not get back if the creek rises. Lucy Mae, honey, you hear me? Stay in, out of the rain."

Lucy Mae nodded above her piece of corn bread. "I'll help here," she said.

Pa pushed back his chair. "I'll go down to the barn

and take care of Maud," he said, reaching for his hat while Lucy Mae hurried to get his canvas coat drying on the chair before the fire, and his big hunting boots. She dragged the boots in, one at a time. Her father, putting them on, hardly stopped to thank her, he was thinking so hard about the rain and the woodpile and Maud.

Pa was proud of the great, black mule. "There isn't a horse nor a mule in the country as good as Maud," he boasted. "Maud's gentle as a kitten and pulls like an army mule."

To the Arkansas farmer, whether of the hill country or the lowlands, his mule is often his chief dependence. In the sparse hill country, the mule sets shoulder to the collar and drags the plow blade through the thin, rocky soil. In the lowlands, the mule treads the cotton rows, nipping gently here and there at a last year's stalk, turning the furrows in even lines. A good mule is the farmer's pride and his partner in raising a crop.

Maud had been on the farm ever since Lucy Mae could remember. Many a time, the little girl had ridden to the field on the big mule, clinging to the plow-lines looped across the broad back and giving them an extra shake to hurry Maud's stride. So she understood, that after caring for his family, Pa's next thought was to go down and look after Maud.

Lucy Mae ran to the window to watch him splashing along down to the barn. Already the flat space where the woodpile had been was a-float with chip boats, washing lazily back and forth on a film of muddy water in thin, eddying currents blown by the wind.

"I wish I could go out and float a chip boat," thought Lucy Mae.

Below the barn slope she could hear the race of the water through the creek. It was early for the creek to rise. Everyone looked for rain in March and April when the floodwaters raced down every gully and the dogwood and redbud trees flaunted spring blossoms under drenched skies. And even in late June there was often rain, filling and flooding the creek and backing up into the garden. That was all part of spring.

But this rushing torrent, growling and snarling as it raced level with the banks on either side, was new and frightening. Muddy waves splashed against the sycamore trees along the bank, and bits of drifting branches tossed on the current like frightened dancers, beckoning for help.

And, worst of all, the creek was almost on a level with the barn, down the little slope where Pa was striding through the rain to look out for Maud. The year before, he had had to move Maud up on the high place back of the house, and he said then he'd better put a new barn there because another high flood might wash away the old one.

Maud was all right, though, he said after he had splashed his way back again. The barn leaked a little where the old pine had fallen on it, but it wouldn't hurt Maud at all. And except that the creek was nearly over the banks, everything was "as snug as a bug under a chip."

"But not the bugs under the chips in our woodpile," said Lucy Mae. "They're swimming for their lives."

"How could it rain so much?" she asked her mother the next day. Hour after hour, the storm grew louder and the rain heavier. Hour after hour, the noise of the rising creek filled the cabin, and Pa looked worried as he piled logs on the fire, or gazed out of the window toward the barn.

Lucy Mae pulled her bed from under the eaves as the drenching torrent soaked through the worn, old shingles and the steady drip-drip of seeping water spattered the loft. Ma handed her the big cooking kettle to put under the biggest leak, and Lucy Mae handed down all the covers from her little bed to be dried before the fire.

She knew Pa was worried. He was staring out of the window again. Then he stirred the fire and dragged on his tall boots to splash down to the barn.

It was just dark when the creek "went out" with a mighty roar of waters. Lucy Mae heard it go; the dull, soft slide of sodden banks and the roar of a released current, spreading far and wide.

Through the chinks of the barn, Pa's lantern threw fingers of light across a muddy river, where a moment ago had been the trampled black mud of the barnyard. An empty chicken coop sailed around slowly on the flood, and through the open barn door drifted a broken barrel, bobbing and curtseying on the floodwaters.

"Ma!" cried Lucy Mae. "Here comes Pa with Maud!" The lantern swung its circle of light across the rising water as Pa led the mule from the barn.

"He's probably going to tie Maud on that high place," said her mother.

But Pa didn't turn toward the high place back of the house. Instead, he brought Maud right up to the front steps. It looked as though the animal would never take

the two steps from the ground to the porch. Ma took the halter and pulled, and Pa pushed, and Lucy Mae danced with excitement, while Maud brayed in a great gust of surprise and bewilderment. But at last the pushing and the pulling brought the mule up on the porch.

"Are you going to bring Maud into the house?" shouted Lucy Mae above the stamping of hoofs and the roar of the creek.

Her father shook his head and tied the animal to the porch post. "She'll be all right there," he said, "but I thought she ought to be under cover." He shook the rain off the brim of his hat. "I think I've never seen such a flood."

Hour after hour through the night, the little cabin shook with the force of the wind while the roar of the creek grew louder and louder.

"We'd better leave," said Ma the next morning when the first light showed the water in the yard almost level with the porch. Under the cabin, the water had risen against the floor boards and the yard was hidden under the rising flood.

"We ought to, but what will we do about Maud?" asked Pa anxiously. "I'll tell you. You and Lucy Mae pack, and I'll go for a boat. Maybe I can ride Maud out to high ground and then row back for you."

It was almost as much work getting the mule off the porch as it had been getting her on the night before, but at last Pa got the animal down, knee-deep in water, and rode away. How Ma and Lucy Mae hurried, packing the big carry-all and the canvas suitcase!

"Don't cry, Ma," begged the child, but her mother cried just the same, because she couldn't take her Rose-of-Sharon quilt—nor the Log Cabin quilt—nor the wild-grape jam—nor the big picture of Grandma and Grandpa in the black and gold frame.

"Better wrap up the corn bread, Lucy Mae, honey," Ma said. "There's no knowing where we'll go, and they might not be expecting company."

But here was Pa back again with Maud splashed and muddy.

"I couldn't get out," he said wearily, dropping off on the porch, while the mule hung a tired head. "I couldn't swim at this end of the creek, and the bridge is out below. You can't tell how deep it is, nor how fast. I guess we're caught in the floodwater. They are all gone at Fred Smith's place, and the water is almost up to the eaves down there."

"Maybe they'll come and look for us," said Ma. But she put her apron over her face.

Pa turned and turned his hat in his hands. "Maybe so," he said softly, and untied the rope from Maud's halter, and slapped the great mule sharply on the flank. "You'll have to swim your way out, Maud," he said sadly.

When help came three days later, Lucy Mae and her parents were in the loft. Around them were piles of household goods, the Rose-of-Sharon quilt and the Log Cabin quilt and the reed-bottomed chairs. Grandma and Grandpa from the black and gold frame smiled fixedly down at them. Below, the floodwaters lapped the stairs, and the floating firewood bumped the ceiling.

A Coast Guard motorboat with Fred Smith in the stern for a guide, rocked just below the window of the loft.

"It was a good thing you saw us waving," called Ma. "I don't think we could have held out much longer."

Pa helped Ma climb over the windowsill into the boat. Lucy Mae said nothing. It was Pa who asked anxiously, "Have any of you seen Maud?"

"No, sir," replied the coast guardsman. "We didn't see anyone all the way from Fred Smith's store."

But Fred knew the answer.

"Maud isn't a person," he explained. "Maud's a mule. That old mule swam down to the highway, and one of the boys found her and rode her down to the store last night. That's how we knew you were still up here," he told Pa. "She hadn't broken her halter, so we guessed that you must have turned her loose to swim."

The coast guardsman picked up Lucy Mae and swung her into the boat. Then Pa climbed in.

"You'll have to leave everything here," warned the

coast guardsman firmly. "But the worst of the flood is over, and your things will be all right until you get back in."

Watching the flying spray, Lucy Mae sat in the bow with the Rose-of-Sharon quilt over her shoulders. Back of her, the water of the creek lapped at the cabin. And down at the crossroads store, Maud was safe and sound.

"I guess everything's all right," said Lucy Mae contentedly, "but I sure will be glad to see Maud."

Mardi Gras

LOUISIANA

"AM I *really* here in New Orleans, or am I dreaming?" Carolyn Lee asked her cousin.

It was the eve of Mardi Gras. The two girls were seated in the front row of the balcony in the large Municipal Auditorium, looking down upon the dancers at the annual Momus Ball.

"You're really here," replied Marie. "But it is like a dream—the people in evening clothes and fancy costumes, and wearing masks—and the orchestra playing. We're so happy that you could come!"

Marie's parents were sitting in the second row just behind the girls. "Indeed, we are," said Mrs. Garnett, Marie's mother, as she leaned over to speak to her niece from Atlanta. "Your mother and I have always said, you know, that you were to come to visit us for Mardi Gras when you and Marie were thirteen."

"Now we've grown up at last," said Carolyn happily.

Mr. Garnett chuckled. "Well, in your new party dresses, you *look* very grown-up. And I'm sure Uncle Maurice and Mathilde will think so."

The girls had not met Mathilde Boyd to whom their

uncle was engaged. She lived in Memphis and was to visit friends in New Orleans for the carnival season. Uncle Maurice had planned to introduce her to his nieces that evening at the ball being given by his Club, and they were looking forward to meeting their future aunt.

"Can you pick out Uncle Maurice?" Mr. Garnett asked Carolyn as she peered down at the gay scene through the opera glasses he had passed to her.

"No," she said. "And, of course, I can't find Mathilde. Oh, there's a lovely colonial lady with a pink hoop-skirt and a white wig. Perhaps—"

"Why, Maurice!" Mrs. Garnett exclaimed suddenly. The girls turned to see their uncle standing there in the aisle of the balcony. He was dressed as a courtier in dark green velvet, and he wore a small black mask. "Where is Mathilde?" asked Mrs. Garnett.

He hesitated. "She—she couldn't come."

"Oh, I'm so sorry!" said Mrs. Garnett.

Marie and Carolyn looked disappointed.

"She changed her plans," said Uncle Maurice. "But come, you girls mustn't look so sad. We'll have a good time. Carolyn, may I have this dance? Marie and I will have the next one."

He drew a small light-blue mask from his pocket. "Here, Carolyn, wear this. All the dancers are masked, you know."

As soon as Uncle Maurice and Carolyn had left, Mr. Garnett said, "He's very disappointed. He'd counted on introducing Mathilde to all his friends at the ball this evening."

"I do wonder what's happened," murmured Mrs. Garnett.

Marie wondered, too, as she sat there looking down at the dancers. She felt sorry for her uncle. Then she happened to glance on the floor of the aisle beside her. She saw a folded telegram. Curiously she picked it up, and almost before she knew it, she had read the few words:

CANNOT ATTEND BALL MOTHER ILL MATHILDE

Then she noticed that it was addressed to Uncle Maurice.

"Oh—!" Marie started to tell her parents. But she realized that her uncle had dropped the telegram by mistake and that she had read this message which was meant only for him. She knew that she must return it to him as soon as possible and say nothing about it to the others. She slipped it into her evening bag.

Mr. and Mrs. Garnett and the girls went home from the ball rather early, but Uncle Maurice stayed on with his friends.

"It's been such a happy evening," declared Carolyn later, as they stepped into the hall of the Garnetts' home. "But, of course, it wasn't so happy for Uncle Maurice."

At the sound of Uncle Maurice's name, there was a high-pitched bark at the head of the stairs—and down bounded Tachette, his little terrier. The girls leaned over to pat the dog, and she licked their hands and barked joyously.

When the girls were upstairs in their room, Carolyn exclaimed, "I think that Mathilde was *very* thoughtless to change her plans."

Remembering the telegram, Marie had a hard time to keep from telling why Mathilde had not come as she had promised.

Just before going to bed, Marie went down the hall to her uncle's room. She sat at his desk and wrote a note which she clipped to the telegram she had brought home. It said:

Dear Uncle Maurice,

I found this at the ball.

Love from Marie

P.S. Carolyn and I had a good time, but we know you didn't—and we're sorry.

The next day was Mardi Gras. The big parade was to be held in the afternoon. After lunch, Marie and Carolyn started off in the car with their uncle to get their costumes. Friends were going to call for Mr. and Mrs. Garnett. They all had reserved places on a grandstand along the line-of-march on Canal Street where more than a hundred thousand people were expected to be watching the parade.

"I can hardly wait to see the floats," Carolyn told her cousin as they squeezed into the front seat of the car beside their uncle. "I've seen so many pictures of the Mardi Gras parade, and now I'm *really* going to see it!"

On the way to the costumer's, Uncle Maurice drove through the Old French Quarter.

"This was the original part of the city, you know," Marie told Carolyn. "It got its name because so many French-speaking people lived here when New Orleans was founded over two hundred years ago."

Uncle Maurice was driving very slowly along the

quaint streets. They were narrow streets, and some of the houses had overhanging balconies, trimmed with beautiful iron railings. Marie and her cousin could look into even narrower passage-ways which led into sunny patios where flowers, palms, and banana trees grew.

They passed antique and curio shops where old furniture, chinaware, and jewelry were on display in the windows. When Uncle Maurice turned the car into one street, the girls got the sweet odor of jessamine as they drove by the open door of a little perfume shop.

On a corner by a lamp-post, an old man stood with a basket on his arm. "Pralines!" he called. "Pralines!" Uncle Maurice stopped to buy a bag of these candy patties made of brown sugar and pecans; he and the girls began munching on them. Farther along, a woman was seated in the doorway of her shop. "Hot meat pies!" she called in a clear, sweet drawl.

A small girl came out of a bakery; she was carrying a long, tapering loaf of French bread under her arm. A man passed by with a top-heavy basket balanced on his head; it was heaped with pineapples.

Suddenly Marie whispered, "Oh, there's a chimney sweep!"

Curiously Carolyn looked at a man dressed in old clothes, and a black top-hat. He carried a coil of rope over one shoulder, and a sheaf of palmetto palms on his back.

"Ramonez la cheminée du haut en bas!" he called out. *"Ramonez—"*

"He says, 'Sweep the chimney from top to bottom,'" Marie explained to her cousin. "He cleans the chimney by letting down the bundle of palms on his rope, and then pulling it up again. But, of course, today he won't really do any work because it's Mardi Gras."

"Oh, I never expected to see a chimney sweep outside of a storybook," said Carolyn as she turned to watch the man strolling across the street.

The sidewalk in front of the costumer's was crowded with maskers in fancy costume on their way to the parade. As Marie and her cousin got out of the car, there was a little yelp from the back seat, and to their surprise Tachette leaped out after them.

"How did she get in there?" Marie asked in dismay.

"She must've jumped in just before we left, and we never knew it," said Carolyn.

Their uncle chuckled. "She didn't want to miss the parade. Come along, Tachette!"

Madame Tureau, the costumer, greeted them at the door. "These are your nieces?" she asked Uncle Maurice. "I have gypsy costumes and little red masks for them. As for you, *m'sieur*—I thought you would enjoy being a pirate."

"Gypsies and a pirate!" exclaimed Marie. "Goody!"

They had soon changed into their costumes and put on their masks.

"Yo, ho, ho for the buccaneer!" Uncle Maurice sang out from behind his false-face. It had a black patch over one eye, and a large nose with a ring in the end of it.

Madame Tureau remarked, "Ah, *m'sieur,* you and your nieces look very gay. And see—I have dressed up your dog, too."

There on the counter stood Tachette with a red ruff around her neck, and a tiny red cap tilted over one ear.

"She looks too sweet for words," said Marie, stroking Tachette.

Uncle Maurice went to park the car in a parking place. When he returned, he tucked the little terrier under his arm and led his nieces through the good-natured, noisy crowds to Canal Street.

Mr. and Mrs. Garnett and their friends were already seated on the grandstand. They laughed when they saw the masked gypsies and the pirate take their places in front of them.

"We searched all over for Tachette," said Marie's mother in a relieved tone when she saw the dog poke her head out from under Uncle Maurice's arm.

The two girls made room for Tachette between them.

People were milling about on the sidewalks and in the street. Many of them were masked and in costume. In a clear space in the middle of the street, a group of

clowns tumbled about while the onlookers shouted with laughter.

Now, from the distance, came a blare of band music. The people in the street moved toward the curbs. Marie and her cousin could see the long line of Mardi Gras floats following the band which was now playing the march, *Pomp and Circumstance*. Gradually, the parade approached as the throngs of people applauded.

"Here comes Rex!" announced Marie.

Rex, the King of the Carnival, rode on the first float which was a large golden throne. Dressed in a white satin robe, covered with pearls, he sat there bowing to left and right. The gems in his crown and scepter glittered in the sunlight. On the steps of the throne, stood little pages in purple velvet costumes, tossing trinkets to the cheering crowds.

"Now come the floats which describe the early history of New Orleans," Uncle Maurice told his nieces as they leaned forward eagerly.

The first one was of shining silver, trimmed with golden *fleurs-de-lis*. Above it fluttered the flags of Spain, France, and the United States which had flown over New Orleans at different periods during its early history.

Now came a float showing the bow of a canoe, with a group of men. They were early explorers. The men stared straight ahead as the float moved along. One of them supported a large cross, bearing the date, 1682.

"He's the French explorer, La Salle," Uncle Maurice told Carolyn. "He and his men came way down the Mississippi to the Gulf of Mexico in 1682. La Salle erected a cross near our present city, and named the territory *Louisiana* in honor of King Louis XIV of France."

The next float was almost hidden by moss-hung branches of cypress trees, but through them could be seen a canoe. Seated in it, were a priest, an Indian with a painted face, holding a tomahawk, and two men wearing leather jackets with fringed sleeves and fur caps.

"Those are some of the men who explored the lower Mississippi River in the early days," said Uncle Maurice. "There's a Jesuit priest and an Indian guide; a Canadian

voyageur, who worked as a boatman or trapper for a fur company in olden times; and a *coureur de bois,* a hunter who traveled over the forest trails of the great American wilderness long before there were any roads."

Loud applause greeted the next float which was a very simple one. It bore only an enormous parchment scroll upon which were inscribed these words:

1718

La Nouvelle Orléans
Founded and Named in Honor of
Philippe, Duc d'Orléans,
the Regent of France

"Louisiana remained a French colony until 1763," Uncle Maurice told the girls as the float moved along. "Then it was ceded to Spain, which had originally claimed the territory. But in 1800, when Napoleon was Emperor of France, he forced Spain to give it back to France, and later he sold the colony to the United States."

Cheers greeted the next float which bore the words:

December 20, 1803
Louisiana Purchase
$15,000,000.

This float presented a colorful scene: a group of people gathered around a flagpole from which was flying the flag of France. There were folks in gay colonial dress, soldiers in French and American uniforms, a sailor with a monkey, Indians with strings of shells over their arms, and fur traders with pelts slung over their shoulders.

"Oh—I know!" cried Marie. "That's the famous scene in the Place d'Armes when the United States took possession of Louisiana!"

"Yes," said Uncle Maurice. "The tricolor, the flag of France, has already been raised in place of the Spanish flag. And now, as we watch—"

"There's the French flag coming down!" said Carolyn.

"And now our flag's being lifted!" exclaimed Marie.

"Through the Louisiana Purchase," concluded Uncle Maurice when the cheers of the crowds had subsided, "the territory of our country was doubled in size. That great section west of the Mississippi River to the Rocky Mountains, from the Gulf of Mexico to the border of Canada, had come into the possession of the new United States of America."

Now followed other floats, showing scenes of present-day New Orleans. A wharf scene moved by. There were bales of cotton and tobacco leaves. Husky stevedores held on their shoulders sacks of coffee and sugar and great stems of bananas. Another float had a cabin made entirely of sugar cane.

Now a hush spread over the spectators as a garden of pink roses approached. In front of an arbor, a group of young women stood about a fountain. They were all dressed in full-skirted costumes of pink satin rose petals. The sparkling jets from the fountain were made of pearls and crystal. One of the young women sat on a settee under the arbor.

"Oh, isn't she beautiful?" exclaimed Marie.

Carolyn said, "I'm sure she's the most beautiful person in the world!"

As they watched the float passing by, Marie suddenly let out a wail, "Oh, there goes Tachette!"

"Tachette!" Uncle Maurice called. But the little terrier had dashed down from the stand and disappeared into the crowds on the sidewalk. Uncle Maurice hurried after her, and the girls hurried after him.

"She's such a little dog to be lost," wailed Marie.

As they elbowed their way along, Marie and her cousin caught glimpses of the rose-garden float moving slowly past. They could hear Tachette's high-pitched bark, but they could not see her.

"Oh, dear, I hope she isn't getting stepped on!" Carolyn's voice was trembling.

Uncle Maurice suddenly laughed. It was the first time he had sounded really cheerful since before the ball. "Come on, gypsies!"

They followed him off the sidewalk and into the street, and then alongside of the rose-garden float.

"There she is!" announced their uncle, pointing at the float.

Seated beside the young woman under the arbor, was the little terrier with the red ruff and the cap tilted over one ear!

That evening, it was a gay family party that gathered in one of the restaurants in the Old French Quarter.

"I was so glad when Uncle Maurice said he wanted to celebrate because Tachette didn't get lost—" began Marie.

Then she and Carolyn gasped, and stared. Coming into the room, was their uncle with the young woman they had seen under the arbor on the rose-garden float!

"This is Mathilde!" Uncle Maurice announced.

"Oh—oh!" That was all Marie and her cousin could seem to say.

Now two waiters were serving dinner. There were delicious things to eat, as Carolyn soon discovered, for wasn't she there in New Orleans, which from the days of the Spanish and French colonists had been famous for its good food?

For this special party, Uncle Maurice had ordered: a rich brown soup with fried, stuffed crayfish heads; oysters baked in the half-shell with a sauce flavored with anchovy; pompano, cooked and served in buttered paper bags; candied yams; artichokes, and avocado salad with cold mushroom sauce.

Looking across at Mathilde, the girls were glad she was going to be their aunt.

During the meal, she explained to them, "Mother is ever so much better. I was able to leave her, but not until it was too late to get here in time for the ball."

"Oh—" Carolyn gasped. "Is that why you didn't come?"

"Yes," Uncle Maurice answered for Mathilde. "Didn't Marie tell you?"

Carolyn stared at her cousin. "You knew—all the time?"

"By accident, I saw the telegram she sent," replied Marie. "But it wasn't for me to tell what was in it."

"Oh—" Carolyn hesitated. Then she said to Mathilde,

"I thought perhaps you changed your plans because you just didn't care about Mardi Gras."

"Not care about Mardi Gras?" Mathilde asked. "Why, I used to live in New Orleans, and even after I moved away I never have missed Mardi Gras. I always come back. This year, my friends, the Bonnells, were arranging a rose-garden float, and they invited me to be on it. I was able to get here just in time for the parade."

Now the waiter served the dessert. It was pie made of light, flaky puff-paste, filled with chocolate cream and with balls of puff-paste on top.

"Tachette seemed to know you in the parade," said Marie.

Uncle Maurice laughed. "Whenever Mathilde comes to visit in New Orleans," he explained, "Tachette always calls on her—with me, of course."

"But it's lucky she recognized you on the float," Carolyn told Mathilde; "or Uncle Maurice might not have seen you. Then he wouldn't have known you'd come for Mardi Gras after all."

Uncle Maurice laughed. "The Bonnells called me up and told me she had come. I knew all the time that Mathilde was on the float, but I wanted to surprise you girls."

"Oh, you did!" exclaimed Marie and Carolyn together.

Star

TEXAS

CLOSE to the Mexican border in southwestern Texas, stretched the wide lands of Sunset Ranch. Herds of cattle bearing the Travers' brand were grazing under the red sky of late-afternoon.

"Well, it's like old times, isn't it?" Barton called over his shoulder as Uncle Steve swung the car into the ten-mile-long dirt road that led to the ranch house.

"Oh, yes!" replied his sister Emily from the back seat where she was sitting beside her aunt. She looked out over the range where the grass seemed to have turned to gold in the light of the western sky. "Vacation time again at Sunset Ranch!"

"And may it be a very happy one," added her aunt who was always glad to have her young niece and nephew from Austin spend the summer at the ranch.

"It will be," Barton assured her. "Golly, I can't think what a vacation would be like unless we were here riding the range."

Uncle Steve chuckled. He and Aunt Verda had driven up to San Antonio to meet the children at the station. "That's the way to talk, cowboy."

"Well, I'm only a city cowboy now," admitted his nephew, "but I'll toughen up."

"So will I," added Emily, eagerly. "We've brought new ten-gallon hats. They ought to help."

At intervals, the ranch was marked off at right angles with barbed-wire fencing. Running parallel with the fencing were wooden gates across the road to keep the roaming cattle within these pastures. As Uncle Steve stopped at each of the gates, Barton hopped out to open it. Then, after the car had passed through, he closed it again and got back into the front seat. The last gate was two miles from the house.

The sun was going down behind the western range,

and the sea of grass turned to dark green with misty blurs where the sage grew.

Now they came to the house with the barns and the bunkhouses where the ranch hands lived. And there was Rosita, the Mexican cook, waving from the kitchen steps. Behind her were her two daughters, Maria and Eugenie, who helped with the housework.

"Buenas tardes (good afternoon)! *Qué lindos niños* (what nice-looking children)! *Qué grandes* (how big)!" these faithful members of the Travers household greeted Emily and her brother in Spanish.

"Do put supper on the table at once, Rosita!" Aunt Verda called. "Something tells me that my niece and nephew are starved."

"How did you guess?" laughed Barton as he carried the suitcases upstairs.

Rosita hurried into the kitchen followed by Maria and Eugenie.

For supper there were tamales (ta mah′ lez)—Indian corn-meal dough rolled around a filling of ground meat and red peppers, and served in cornhusks in which they had been steamed. Rosita had also made tortillas (tor teé yaz), flat pancakes of mashed corn. There were small pitchers of melted butter, and glasses of buttermilk, and for dessert, fresh figs.

The early evening air was sweet with sage as Emily and her brother walked over to the barns.

"Hello!" called a familiar voice. "Hello!" It was the tall, white-haired Old Ranger, the foreman at Sunset Ranch. He had been given the nickname, *Old Ranger,* because in earlier days he had helped keep law and order there in the cattle country of the Southwest when bands of outlaws and rustlers roamed the great ranch lands.

"I heard you'd come," he drawled after greeting the children.

"We want to see Star right away," Barton told him eagerly.

"And Bonita," added Emily.

The two cow ponies seemed to be waiting for their old friends. Star was all black with a white star on his forehead just between the eyes. Bonita was reddish brown with a white sock on her right hindfoot. They nickered and nuzzled their noses into the children's hands.

"Finest ponies on the ranch," remarked Old Ranger. "Why don't you ride 'em at the Rodeo in August?"

"Rodeo?" laughed Barton. "Are you joking?"

"We're just two softies from the city," Emily reminded him.

"You'll harden up on the range," said Old Ranger. "There haven't been any young riders in the Travers family since your uncle was a boy here on the ranch. Now's your chance to show what the Travers name stands for here in the cattle country. You can enter the

races for young riders of cow ponies. Of course, you'll have some stiff competition. Those youngsters up at the Diamond T Ranch were raised in the saddle, and Cowboy Ike was telling me today they're goin' in."

He ran his hand down Star's neck, and patted Bonita on the shoulder.

"There're no better junior riders than those young folks at Diamond T," he said in his careful drawl, "but there's no cow pony I've seen in the county who can hold a candle to these two here at Sunset. A good pony's half the battle."

"Well, if we do decide to go in," said Emily as they

left the barn to return to the house, "let's make it a big surprise for Aunt Verda and Uncle Steve."

"They'd be proud if you won," was Old Ranger's comment. "The first rodeo prize in the Travers family since—"

"Hold on," laughed Barton. "We haven't agreed we'd go in yet, have we, Emily?"

"Sh-sh," warned Emily. "Here comes Uncle Steve."

And so began the long summer at Sunset Ranch.

Part of each day was spent out on the range where the world seemed made up of only sky and the wide reaches of the green grass. Hour upon hour, the children rode with the cowboys who were rounding up the cattle. Under the blazing sun, they tanned and freckled. In the high-pommeled saddles, their muscles strengthened as they rode with the rhythm of their ponies.

"Well," drawled the Old Ranger one evening along in August, "I've been watching you pretty carefully, and I've come to the conclusion that you can handle those two cow ponies just about as cleverly as any young riders I've seen."

He stopped talking, and they listened to the frogs croaking in the pond down by the corral. The children knew what he was going to say.

"What about the Rodeo?" he asked. "It's only a week off, you know."

"We haven't forgotten what you told us that first night we were here at Sunset," said Emily. "About Aunt Verda and Uncle Steve being proud of us, I mean, if we did go in and win. And we've been thinking a lot about it, haven't we, Bart?"

"Yes, we have," declared her brother. "We think we're toughened up enough for it now, and we've decided to go in—"

"That's fine!" boomed the Old Ranger.

"But we don't expect to win," Emily hurried on to explain. "Not with those Diamond T Ranch boys in the same race. But we're going in, just for the fun of it."

The evening before the Rodeo, they were sitting on the wide veranda of the ranch house. It had been a hot day, but now a cool breeze blew from the northern range, rustling the grass.

The Old Ranger told stories of the days when, as a young man, he had "ridden the fences," patrolling the long stretches of barbed-wire boundaries of the ranches, ever on the alert for cattle thieves and outlaws.

Uncle Steve talked about the earlier days his grandfather used to tell about when the trail drivers of Texas drove the great wild herds to the far-distant railroad shipping-points in Kansas and Missouri—"sometimes more than a thousand miles away." He told how in one period of only fifteen years, over five million heads of cattle had been driven to market out of the state.

"Of course," he concluded, "that was before the railroads reached Texas."

Then Aunt Verda announced abruptly, "You children should be turning in. It's getting late. We'll all want to drive over to the Fairgrounds tomorrow, I suppose?"

"That's so," drawled the Old Ranger, getting up to leave. "Tomorrow's the Rodeo. I'd almost forgotten."

Emily and her brother nudged each other. Their aunt and uncle didn't even suspect that they were going in the races.

The following day was bright and sunny.

"Real rodeo weather," observed the Old Ranger when he greeted the children out in the barn where Cowboy Ike had just finished currying the two ponies. "Are you ready for the big ride?"

"Don't we look it?" Emily asked while her brother laughed.

"I'll say you do," he drawled. He looked down at their high boots, khaki breeches, gay plaid shirts of green and pink, purple bandannas, and ten-gallon hats. "You'll scare the other ponies off the track," he chuckled.

Cowboy Ike joined in while he saddled Star. Then he said seriously, "Watch out for those boys from the Diamond T. I hear they do some pretty rough ridin'. Better lose a pony's length at the start of the race than get mixed up with them."

"I'll watch out," declared Barton. "Thanks, Ike."

"You needn't worry about me," added his sister. "I'll be too far behind to get mixed up with the Diamond T ponies."

"Now, now, don't talk that way," said the Old Ranger good-naturedly. "Do your best, Emily. Bonita's a better pony than the ones they'll ride. As for Star, here—" he held the bridle while Cowboy Ike saddled Emily's pony—"well, Bart, I think he's apt to do a shade better than Bonita. Your uncle was offered a good price for Star the other day. But he wouldn't sell him. 'He's my nephew's pony,' was the only answer he made."

Barton's eyes shone. He patted the pony on the shoulder, and Star pawed the ground restlessly.

"I'd like to win," he said simply. "If Uncle Steve feels that way about Star."

"Oh, I hope you do win," his sister told him.

They rode the ten miles to the Fairgrounds—Emily and Barton and the Old Ranger and Cowboy Ike. Aunt Verda and Uncle Steve followed later in the car.

A great crowd had already arrived before them: Texas cowboys and ranchmen, Mexican *vaqueros* (cowboys) with *sarapes* (small blankets) slung over their shoulders, men and women and children, and young cowboys and cowgirls from neighboring ranches. Emily and her brother stayed with the Old Ranger and Cowboy Ike at one side of the Fairgrounds, near the stables. Opposite them was the grandstand with flags flying, and in the front row—Aunt Verda and Uncle Steve.

Now things got under way. There was tense excitement in the air. The brass band played *The Eyes of Texas Are Upon You.* After a flourish on the cornets, a long line of cowboys and steer ropers, shouting and whistling, appeared on the racetrack and made a complete circle as they rode their horses around the ring.

They were dressed in gay vests, studded with brilliants, and angora chaps of blue and orange and green. They waved their sombreros, or wide-brimmed hats, to the cheering spectators. The sunlight flashed on bridles and spurs. Lassos whirled, and the beat of the horses' hoofs sounded over the ground.

After the dust had settled, there came a *r-r-r-r-rumble* of drums, and a man in a ten-gallon hat stood up before a microphone in front of the band and announced:

"Ladies and gentlemen! We will now have the first race! A half-mile race for bareback riders! Once around the ring!"

Out into the track came a crowd of whooping cowboys on horses with no saddles. At the crack of a pistol off started the bareback riders around the track. One by one, they were joggled off their horses, as the crowd yelled and jeered. The winner had hardly any competition at all for the simple reason that almost all the other riders had fallen off their horses.

Next, a bucking bronco, with a saddle but no rider, was led out into the corral in the center of the ground enclosed by the track. He bucked and reared and squealed. Then a cowboy ran up to him and struggled to mount the animal while he ducked and pitched. The cowboy did succeed in getting into the saddle, and no matter how the bronco bucked and reared, the cowboy seemed glued to the seat. Finally, the animal quieted down and the cowboy rode out of the corral with a jubilant *"whoop-la-whoop!"*

Now, out of the stables and into the corral, came three cowboys, each riding backwards and bareback on a bellowing, bucking steer. The riders managed to hang on for a while, and the spectators shouted, "Attaboy! Hang on, cowboy!" But before long, the steers returned to the stables, leaving the three riders seated on the ground, to the wild merriment of the crowd.

While the band played a Sousa march, venders of popcorn and lemonade shouted their wares as they made their way up and down the steps of the grandstand.

Then came another announcement from the man in the ten-gallon hat:

"Ladies and gentlemen! We will now see the mile race for cowboys! Twice around the ring!"

Intent on watching the cowboys get into position for the start of this famous race in which the best riders of the county always competed, Emily and Barton climbed up on the low wire fence on the outer edge of the track. They hooked the heels of their riding boots in an opening a few inches above the ground, and sat down, only keeping their balance because of the wooden post between them. They heard the crack of the pistol, and they cheered with the crowd.

"Look at 'em go!" shouted Cowboy Ike.

Then it happened—and it turned into a rodeo that the Travers family never forgot. The wire suddenly gave way, and Emily and her brother lost their balance. The Old Ranger caught Emily before she fell—but Barton slid over backwards, with his foot caught in a loop of the wire.

"Are you hurt, son?" Cowboy Ike leaned over him and freed the riding boot from the fence. Then he helped Barton to sit up.

The boy did not reply at once. He gritted his teeth. "My—my ankle hurts," he said.

"Oh, Bart!" Emily stood there with tears in her eyes. "You mean—"

"I mean—I can't ride Star," replied her brother huskily.

"Can't ride—Star?" she gasped. "Oh—why—Old Ranger, what will we do?"

The Old Ranger was removing the boy's boot. He had it off now and was examining Barton's ankle, carefully, gently, with his big hands.

"Maybe just a strain," he drawled. "But anyway—there's no riding in the Rodeo for you."

"Oh!" exclaimed Emily. "After your wanting to win—to make Uncle Steve proud—oh—"

The spectators were cheering. She heard the pounding of horses' hoofs. Dust blew from the track into her tear-stained face. Then she heard the Old Ranger saying, "It's up to you, Emily. You've got to ride Star. Now, now, no arguments. It's up to you, cowgirl. What d'you say, Bart?"

Barton grinned. "Go to it, Emily! Show the stuff you're made of!"

She squared her chin. "I will!" she declared. "I'll do my best—for you, Bart."

"That's the way to talk," said the Old Ranger. "Now, remember what Ike told your brother. Better lose a length at the start than get mixed up with those ponies from the Diamond T."

The race for the cowboys was over. The band was playing again. The dust settled. Then the announcer called:

"Ladies and gentlemen! We will now see the half-mile race for junior cowboys and cowgirls! Young riders under fourteen! Once around the ring!"

Waiting for the crack of the pistol, Emily held Star there in the line. Then came the signal—they were off!

Star wanted to lead at once, but she held him back.

She glanced to the right. There were the two boys from the Diamond T trying to crowd her toward the outer edge of the track. Sharply, she checked Star and let them cross in front of her. "Better lose a length at the start," she whispered into Star's ear.

Thump-thump-thump-thump! the beating hoofs went around the ring. Emily felt the hot, heavy breathing of ponies all around her—heard the shouts of the other young riders. She and Star were in the middle of it all. Now the ponies were bunched. Then they were strung out in a line—twelve of them. Star was fifth.

Thump-thump-thump-thump! Emily knew she would never forget the beat of those hoofs. She saw a chance

to go ahead of two ponies who were tiring. She guided Star over toward the inner edge.

Thump-thump-thump-thump! It seemed as though she had never heard any other sound but the beat of the hoofs.

"Out in front," she whispered. Star took his stride. A small, brown-and-white pony was edging up close behind them. Emily glanced back. It was one of the Diamond T boys. Star didn't like that! He speeded up.

Thump-thump-thump-thump!

Around the curve now, and into the home stretch. Emily guided Star to the very inner edge of the track. The Diamond T boy was still close behind. Then out went Star's neck and his hoofs flew across the ground. How the crowd was cheering! The grandstand was a blur.

Thump-thump-thump-thump! Emily glanced back. The Diamond T boy had dropped behind. Star was still third.

"Faster, faster!" she whispered into his ear. He overtook the pony in front. Now he was second.

Thump-thump——thump-thump!

Oh, the glorious, thrilling beat of the hoofs! Emily leaned forward for the last dash. Star moved nearer to the leading pony. Inch by inch, he overtook him—and when Emily rode past the judge's box, Star had won by two lengths!

The beat of the hoofs were still in her ears as she turned toward the stables. The spectators were shouting, "Bravo, cowgirl! Bravo!"

The Old Ranger, Cowboy Ike, and Barton were waiting for her. And other cowboys from Sunset Ranch crowded around.

"Good work, Emily," drawled the Old Ranger as she dismounted and he took the bridle. "Real Travers, that's what you are."

"Oh, Bart—" She looked at her brother.

"Don't talk about me," he grinned. "You've put me in the shade. Honest, when I saw you ridin' around that track like a streak o' lightning—well," he gulped.

Late that evening, they all were sitting out on the veranda. The moon was full. In the distance, lights gleamed in the windows of the bunkhouses. From one of them came the music of a concertina.

Emily had set her prize on the table. It was a bronze figure of a Texas longhorn, mounted on a plaque. Barton fondled the prize that Star had won. It was a bridle, with silver trimmings.

Sometimes people are too happy to speak. That's the way it was with the Travers family, the night after the Rodeo.

The Arrow

OKLAHOMA

AS the bus stopped there at the Salt Lick Reservation in Oklahoma, Evelyn Grant and her brother, Robert, stepped out and looked across at the handsome stone house where their Osage Indian friends lived. High above the red maples on the lawn, and high above the roof and the chimneys, towered the three black open-work derricks with the oil pumps keeping up their incessant din: *Pop-pop-chug, pop-pop-chug, pop-pop-chug.*

"I don't see Tom White Crow!" shouted Robert through the noise. "Shall we walk on home?"

The bus that had brought the children over from school at Elk Creek, eight miles away, was quickly disappearing down the road.

"Guess we might as well!" Evelyn called in reply.

They often got off the bus there at the corner to spend the rest of the afternoon with Tom White Crow and his sister, Tallulah Rainbow, who went to the government school on the Reservation. Usually their Indian friends were there to greet them.

"Perhaps they drove somewhere with Creeping Bear!" Robert shouted.

Their father, Creeping Bear, was an expert on locating oil. He traveled throughout the state, advising people where to erect derricks, and he often took his son and daughter with him.

Evelyn and Robert gave a final glance at the house which stood there sedately in the midst of the confusion. Then they turned away to take the short cut home across the large field dotted with tall derricks. Most of them belonged to Indians upon whose allotments of land, oil had been discovered.

The warm October air was heavy with the odor of smoke and oil, and the ground throbbed with the pulsing

of the pumps: *Pop-pop-chug, pop-pop-chug, pop-pop-chug.*

Suddenly, Evelyn and her brother heard a whistle behind them. Quickly, they turned to see Tom White Crow beckoning to them from the yard. They started back toward Tom's house.

"I didn't see you get off the bus," their black-haired friend greeted them. "There's a surprise for you in the house. Come on inside."

"What?" queried Robert in fun, making believe he had not caught the young Indian's words above the chugging of the oil-well pumps.

Tom laughed. The boys often joked about the noise outside the house. Then he tilted back his head and looked up dreamily at the three tall derricks, rising one hundred and twenty feet in the air.

"Father says the oil wells don't seem noisy to him," he declared. "He says they make music."

His friends looked up, too. There rose the graceful frames of steel against the blue sky and the white clouds. *Pop-pop-chug, pop-pop-chug, pop-pop-chug.* Beyond the yard, loomed other derricks belonging to Creeping Bear.

"I know you love those derricks," Evelyn said as they walked toward the house. "But it's hard for us to feel as you do, Tom. We love our farm, you know."

At the back door, Tallulah Rainbow's face appeared, framed by shining black braids. She called out:

"Fresh doughnuts, nice and hot—
Step inside and eat a lot!"

"Thank you, we will!" Eagerly, Evelyn and her brother accepted the invitation.

Tom laughed. "I told you there was a surprise."

The door closed out some of the din of the derricks. There on the table in the large neat kitchen, was a platter heaped with sugared doughnuts; there was a pitcher of milk, too, and glasses.

"Miss Sears gave us the recipe today in Home Making Class," explained Tallulah as they gathered around for an afternoon snack, "and I wanted to try it right away."

Tallulah's doughnuts were delicious, and they were soon gone—all except two. The Indian girl was saving them as a surprise for her mother, Floating Cloud, when she returned from Elk Creek where she had driven to do some shopping.

Later, when Evelyn and Robert were leaving, Tom said, "Before you go, Father wants to speak to you."

They followed him into the richly furnished library, lined with books from the floor to the ceiling. Creeping Bear sat at his mahogany desk by one of the wide windows. Beyond the dark-blue velvet window drapes, the children could see the derricks off on the main oil field and, in the railroad yards, the long rows of tank cars standing on the tracks.

"Please tell your father that I'm coming over to see him this evening," said the quiet-spoken Indian. "It's very important that I have a talk with him."

"We'll tell Dad," Robert assured him. He knew that his father had great respect for Creeping Bear who was an old boyhood friend.

Again outside, with the din of the pumps in their ears, Evelyn and her brother headed for home.

"I wonder why Creeping Bear wants to talk with Dad?" said Evelyn as they passed a slimy-looking slush-pit where the waste from some of Creeping Bear's oil wells was deposited.

"I don't know," Robert admitted. "But it must be very important, if he says so."

Leaving Creeping Bear's allotment where its sixteen wells were all pumping furiously, they followed an old Indian trail. It crossed one corner of the large oil field and skirted the edge of the railroad yards. There were no houses to be seen—only the scattered shacks and tool sheds belonging to some of the workers, most of whom lived at Elk Creek and drove out to the field in their cars.

Everywhere were the tall derricks. There on the level, grassy, treeless land of the Reservation, covering it as far as the children could see, were the giant black frame-works, towering into the hazy blue of the late afternoon. The earth vibrated with their incessant pumping: *Pop-*

pop-chug, pop-pop-chug, pop-pop-chug. The air was filled with their continual roar. The strong smell of smoke and oil clung to the light breeze.

Robert and his sister reached the edge of the railroad yards where the lines of tank cars were strung out on the tracks. Now came the shriek of a steam locomotive in the distance, and down a clear stretch of track which shone like gold in the sun, rushed a lone, black double-header, belching smoke.

"Come on!" shouted Robert.

As they often did when walking home from Tom White Crow's, they climbed nimbly up a few rungs on a small abandoned derrick at the side of the track and watched the engines coming toward them. With clanging bell and hissing steam, the double-header slowed down and passed the derrick where Evelyn and her brother were standing, leaning against the frame. They waved to one of the firemen and then watched the puffing engines switch about some of the oil tanks waiting there on the tracks.

The full tank cars were moved into one long line, and the "empties" onto a sidetrack where they would be filled from the underground pipe running between the huge reserve tanks and the railroad yards. Clang of bell, hiss of steam, rattle of couplings. This was a noisy world, and it trembled with the pounding of the pumps: *Pop-pop-chug, pop-pop-chug, pop-pop-chug.*

After the engineers had finished the switching about, the double-header picked up the long line of full tanks to haul them away to the refineries—the first step in the journey that would take the oil to many parts of the world.

"Eighty-nine!" called Robert as the last of the tank cars rolled past the de ick.

They waved to a trainman standing at the door of the disappearing caboose. Then they climbed down and walked away from the yards.

Later, when they went through the gate in the wire fence that marked the boundary of their own property next to the Reservation, the din of the derricks had dropped into the distance. There they were in their own peaceful pasture where the Jersey cows grazed in the gathering dusk. The children herded them toward the barn lot and into their stalls where they would be milked by electric power.

Mr. Grant was waiting for Robert and Evelyn at the barn.

"Creeping Bear's coming over to see you this evening, Dad," Robert told him promptly. "He says it's something important."

Mr. Grant looked beyond the pasture to where the derricks were outlined against the horizon. "I was going to drive over to the Grange meeting at Elk Creek," he remarked thoughtfully. "But, of course, I'll stay home if Creeping Bear wants to see me especially."

After milking the cows, Robert and his father put the milk through the separator. Then they fed the calves and hogs while Evelyn fed the chickens and the turkeys. As the eggs had already been gathered, there were no more chores to be done before supper, and Mr. Grant and the children strolled over to the house.

It was a rambling, white wooden house with wide porches. There were maple trees on the lawn, and flower beds of yellow chrysanthemums and great shaggy dahlias. The air was cool now at the close of day. The smell of apples came from the near-by orchard.

"I'm glad we haven't any oil derricks in the middle

of our lawn," declared Evelyn as they scuffled through the fallen red leaves at the side of the house.

"I am, too," admitted her brother. "Golly, what a racket those pumps make."

Mr. Grant chuckled as he opened the door. "Your mother and I always say they wouldn't sound very home-like to us."

That evening, the children had just finished their homework in the living room with its open fire, when a car stopped in front of the house.

"I guess that's Creeping Bear." Their mother set aside the book she had been reading.

Mr. Grant went to the front door. "Toss another log on the fire, Robert," he said.

Robert lifted a log from the basket at the side of the hearth, and glanced at his sister. They were both excited, wondering why Creeping Bear wanted to talk with their father. Creeping Bear often came to call, but this was the first time he had told them ahead of time that he was coming.

The flames in the fireplace were leaping merrily when the tall Indian walked into the room. He shook hands with Mrs. Grant and smiled at the children.

"Bob," he said to Mr. Grant when they had drawn their chairs up in front of the hearth, "you've often told me about different people coming here to try and locate oil."

The children's father laughed. "It's a family joke with us—folks coming to hunt for oil in our cabbage beds."

"I believe they've been over every foot of the pasture," added Mrs. Grant, "and all over our twenty-five acres of truck farm, too."

"But not over our front lawn," Evelyn declared hastily, and even Creeping Bear laughed.

Then he spoke seriously. "This morning, Bob, I took my seismograph (size′ mo graf) crew over your south 'eighty.' I consider there are several likely places for drilling."

Robert and Evelyn knew that a seismograph was an instrument used in prospecting for oil.

"You mean—you think there's *really* oil here on our property?" questioned Mrs. Grant in amazement.

Eagerly, Evelyn and her brother waited for the Indian's reply.

"Yes, I believe there is oil," he stated, "and in abundance—especially by the old log corral. If you want to sign the lease papers tonight, Bob—" Creeping Bear drew a long envelope from his coat pocket. "—my men can begin work tomorrow on the derrick."

"A derrick!" exclaimed the children.

For a few moments the only sound in the room was the crackling of the fire.

Then Mr. Grant said quietly, "Yes, Creeping Bear, I'll sign the lease papers to your oil company."

The Indian took the forms from the envelope, and together the men studied them. Then the papers were signed and Creeping Bear drove away.

Fortunately for the children, the next day was Saturday. Right after breakfast, they went out to the old corral with their father. Creeping Bear and Tom White Crow were already there.

"I hear you're going to have some noise around here," said the Indian boy in fun. For once, Robert did not join in their joking. This was serious—a derrick on the Grants' farm!

Soon a truck drove up, bringing workers. Then came other trucks loaded with building materials for the construction of the derrick: sand, gravel, cement, tools; steel girding, huge bolts; lumber, giant drills, tons of casing, and pipe.

"The old pond over there will make a natural slush-pit," Creeping Bear told Mr. Grant as they watched the activities of the workers. "We'll have to spend only a little time on that part of the job."

It took a month to erect the derrick. Every day after school, Robert and his sister came out to the corral to see what progress was being made. They stayed until it was time to do the farm chores before supper. Their mother often came out, too, and Tom White Crow and Tallulah Rainbow, as well as Floating Cloud.

"I don't think any derrick in Oklahoma ever had so much attention," chuckled Mr. Grant one afternoon as they were all watching the men at work.

Carefully, foot by foot, the immense derrick was built into the air. The men worked hard and called loudly to each other through the confusion. As the framework climbed higher, they appeared smaller up there on the girders. There was dust and grease, and pounding and grinding. The sharp clash of steel rang out sharply over the pasture.

At last, there stood the majestic black structure silhouetted against the sky.

"Shall we name it *The Arrow?*" asked Creeping Bear

with pride in his voice, as they looked up at the derrick rising more than a hundred feet above them.

"The Arrow!" the children shouted. "Oh, yes—*The Arrow!"*

Then began the days of drilling for oil. Creeping Bear spent most of his time there, despite his many duties elsewhere. At first, he was in good spirits. But as the days passed and no oil seemed forthcoming, he began to appear anxious.

"Don't take it so hard," the children heard their father say to his Indian friend one afternoon. They had returned from school and found the two men talking in the living room. "There's always the possibility that oil *won't* be found."

"I know," said Creeping Bear, mournfully. "But I was so sure this time—"

"Please—" Mrs. Grant interrupted, coming into the room with cups of coffee on a tray for the men, and cocoa for Evelyn and Robert. "Don't go worrying yourselves over that oil. My goodness, Creeping Bear, this farm is really all we need."

"But I was so sure," repeated the Indian, setting down his cup of coffee. "This is a terrible disappointment, Bob—"

The words were no sooner spoken than a terrific explosion sounded from down in the pasture: B-O-O-O-M!

They all rushed to the front door and looked out.

A tall column of black oil was belching toward the top of the derrick!

"A gusher!" Creeping Bear shouted. "Come on! But keep at a safe distance until we get it capped!"

One week later, the pumps were installed. *Pop-pop-chug, pop-pop-chug, pop-pop-chug!* And the men strung rows of electric lights on the framework.

That evening in the living room, Mrs. Grant said to the children's father, "Well, when your grandfather staked out this claim after the run in '89, he never thought that one day oil would be discovered under his pasture."

"It's happened," admitted Mr. Grant, "thanks to Creeping Bear and his modern ideas. But I have some modern ideas, too—about farming. Now we'll have extra money to buy one of the most up-to-date tractors on the market, for one thing, and Robert's going to learn to run it."

The boy looked at him with shining eyes. "Honest, Dad?"

"Yes, and I have other plans, too, about your education, so you can get an early start in progressive farming. This state will always need cornfields as well as oil fields, Robert, and rows of potatoes as well as rows of derricks. Now—"

"Do come here!" Evelyn's voice held a note of wonder.

The others went over to the window where she was standing. Outside, in the clear night, was *The Arrow,* ablaze for the first time. With its lights twinkling off and on, the derrick was a bejeweled tower, beautiful indeed to see.

The Mission Bell

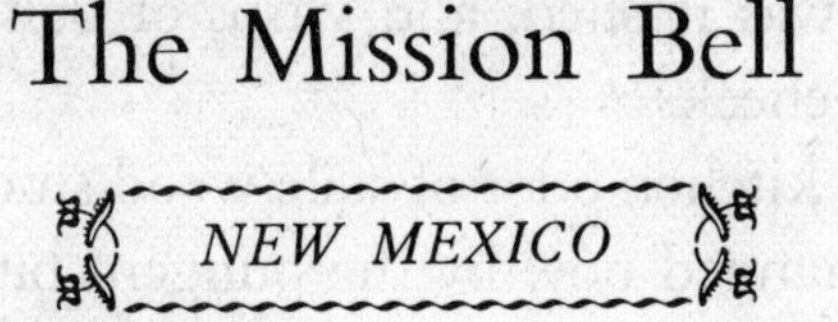

THE Mission bell was ringing in the little New Mexico village of Las Trampas. For over two hundred years the big mellowed bell had called from the belfry of the thick-walled adobe Mission. No one knew how long ago this bell was cast in Spain, shipped to Mexico, and brought by oxcart from Mexico City through hostile Indian desert, across mountain passes and shifting white sands, to be hung in this Mission.

The huge building stood, like a great hen, hovering over its brood of small flat-topped mud houses. In the crisp mountain air the music of the bell sounded clear. On this bright sunny afternoon the little village, where a feeling of excitement had been felt for days, was now stirred into a hustle and bustle at the sound of the bell.

In one of the mud houses Señora Romero was toasting chili peppers over the wood stove in her kitchen. She spoke to her son in the soft tones of old Spanish.

"Those people, your friends Ashleys, are very late to come to *la fiesta* (fee és ta), no, Lupe?" she asked. With a flip of her hand, she brushed the toasted chili peppers from the top of the hot stove onto a folded cloth. Her brown face was flushed, and wisps of damp black hair clung to her cheeks.

The usual kitchen odor of stale wood smoke and dried herbs was changed now by the pungent bite of peppers, the tang of mutton stewing with onions, the smell of hot grease, and of ground beef balls bouncing and bubbling in their own soup.

But Guadalupe (gwah dah loo′ pay), or Lupe, as he was called, did not notice. A streak of August sunlight slanted through the window and glistened upon his slick blue-black hair while he stood watching the narrow dirt road from Truchas.

"There are two roads from Santa Fé," continued Señora Romero. Carefully smothering the warmed chili peppers in the cloth, she placed them in the oven to steam off the skins, and closed the door with a snap. "Maybe your friends, they came through Peñasco and are already at the church with your papá, Sara, Rosa, Marie, and Agapito (ah gah pee′toe)."

"No, I have just been to the church," replied twelve-year-old Guadalupe. Like his mother, he spoke in old Spanish. "They are not there."

His mother looked out of the door to see for herself. But she, too, saw only the scattered houses of the village, golden in the sunlight, and the weed-grown banks of the winding water-ditch.

A neighbor was opening her outdoor clay oven shaped like a bee-hive, and taking out loaves of bread on a paddle. The smell made Señora Romero sniff. Her own bread was still baking in her outdoor oven.

"You are sure your friends are coming?" she insisted.

"Oh, yes," declared Lupe. "When I sold them my little carved chests at the fair in Santa Fé, Mr. Ashley said he would like to bring his children to our village on August twenty-third for the candlelight procession on the eve of our Patron Saint's day. Charles, who is my age, cried out, 'Oh, boy, that's great!' Ann, a bit younger, began to dance around. 'I can scarcely wait for that day!' she said. They were very happy about it. I'm sure they will come."

"I know," said Señora Romero. "It was good that you invited them to visit us. They are very nice people, no? You tell me that they live in Santa Fé only for this summer. They live all the time in some other place?"

"Yes, Mamá," replied her son patiently. "They have never been to New Mexico until this summer. They live in a big city—I do not remember the name. They like our country very much and Mr. Ashley says that every summer they will come back here. They have friends in Santa Fé. They have been to many places, and they will go to California and see the big ocean before they go home again." Lupe sighed.

The boy's mother knew what that sigh meant. She

knew how he had gazed at the map of the United States in his geography and blurted out that he wished he could see the Grand Canyon, Niagara Falls, even the great Carlsbad Caverns in his own state. She knew how he looked longingly at the broad blue oceans on the map, wondering what they were like, and wanting to go and see for himself.

"Lupe," she thought, "is too ambitious. He wants too much the travel to see places, and the learning in books!" She, too, wanted to sigh for him.

Instead, she half-scolded him, "You make yourself unhappy over nothings! You do not see all the good things around you: This nice house your great-great-great-great grandfather built when he came up from Mexico with General De Vargas; this nice ranchito with good water-ditches; your horse and sheep and your papá's cows; the silver spoons the Governor Peralta used himself; and your many trips in the wagon to Santa Fé to sell long strings of chili peppers and apples and your little carved chests! You are not the one to be unhappy, my son. Let other people have the seeing of the ocean, you have plenty."

Señora Romero looked at Lupe's sadly frowning face, above his tight light-blue suit, and she added in softer tones, "If the Ashleys do not come soon, they will miss the vespers. Your papá has been ringing the Mission bell already a long time now, no?"

"I will ask Father Ambrosius to wait a little longer before he begins." Guadalupe made three leaps for the door.

Holding the bottom of his flapping coat as he ran, the boy dodged in and out among the people who were standing in patient groups or walking slowly toward the Mission.

A group of Indians had just arrived in an automobile. Stepping out of the car, they shook hands limply, as was their custom, with their Las Trampas friends who smiled graciously in greeting. As he ran past, Lupe glimpsed the gay calico shawls thrown over the heads of the Indian women, and their big-topped moccasins.

All eyes turned to follow him, for everyone in the

village knew that he was expecting Anglo visitors from Santa Fé for the fiesta. (The Spanish-American people of New Mexico always call all other white people of European descent "Anglos.") Now, as Lupe hurried past them, they began to talk in whispers about what might have happened to his visitors. Secretly, they were glad of the delay, for it dragged out longer the happy hours of anticipation and the joy of being dressed up.

When Lupe rushed into the church, his father asked a silent question with his eyes, as he continued to pull on the heavy bell rope. Lupe answered the look with a shake of his head and hastened into the sacristy to find the padre (priest).

In his brown cassock, Father Ambrosius was slowly pacing back and forth on the clay floor of the dimly-lighted, high-ceilinged room. Here it was cool and musty smelling. Blue shadows played on the plastered walls. The padre looked up as the boy entered.

Speaking in English, he asked anxiously, "Still your friends have not arrived?"

"No, Father. Something must have happened to delay them," Lupe answered between short gasps of breath. "Can you wait—just a little longer for vespers?"

"Yes, my son. This is an important occasion for you. We'll wait."

When Guadalupe had left the room, the padre began to pace back and forth again. "That boy is a fine lad, with a good mind. I wish he might have the chance of travel and education which he wants so badly and deserves so much," he thought. His face brightened. "Something may develop for him," he said aloud. "We'll see." Suddenly, he stepped to the door. "Lupe!" he called.

"Yes, sir!" replied the boy, coming back into the room.

Speaking now in Spanish, the padre explained, "There was a heavy rainstorm in the mountains as I came up at noon today. The two dry washes which the road crosses this side of Truchas must have been running shortly afterward. Your friends are strangers to this country. They do not know the danger of crossing through storm water in an arroyo. They may have difficulty there."

"They may be stuck—they may have lost their car," said Guadalupe. "They may even have—drowned!" he added, his voice trembling. "I had better go to find out—and to help."

"Yes," agreed Father Ambrosius. "Hurry! The procession will wait until you return."

Outside in the sunny plaza stood wagons, filled with chairs and blankets. The wagons had brought visitors from neighboring ranches. The horses, now tethered to the wagon wheels, were munching on hay.

Near-by stood saddled horses with their bridle reins hanging from their bits to the ground. There was no time for Guadalupe to look for his own horse. He dashed for

the saddled pony he knew was fastest and strongest.

"Tony!" he called to a lad sitting on the low mud wall. "I'm going to use your horse to go look for my friends at the arroyo. Come on, fellows!"

Five boys came racing for their horses and jumped into the saddles. The pealing Mission bell made a challenging accompaniment to the rapid beat of horses' hoofs on the dirt road. The riders dashed past patches of dusty corn, chili pepper plants, alfalfa and wheat, and then past low-growing evergreens dotting the rolling hills.

A few minutes later, when they drew rein at the brow of a steep decline, they checked their ponies in horror at what they saw below them—an automobile stranded in the middle of a swift-running arroyo! The red muddy water dashed up over its hood and lashed against the side and top of the car. Three figures were rolling and struggling in a desperate effort to find a footing against the angry current which foamed and swirled about them.

"It's my friends!" shouted Lupe, sticking his heels into the flanks of his horse.

"Come on!" yelled one of the boys.

The ponies went slipping and skidding down the hill, sending stones clattering from under their hoofs.

Down the bank of the arroyo, into the rushing water, the boys urged the balking horses. Once in the water, they fought against the force of the current. The ponies' lips curled back, showing their teeth, and their eyes rolled, showing the whites, as red foam splashed against their manes and shoulders, drenching them. Still their young riders urged them on toward the three struggling people who were rapidly being carried downstream.

It was a grim fight, but the horses and their riders won. Reaching the three in the water, who had somehow managed to cling together, the riders reached out and caught them by their clothing. This gave them the help they needed to get, and hold, a footing. Then, pressing against the straining horses and held firmly by the riders, the struggling people—Mr. Ashley and Charles and Ann—were dragged out of the swift-running stream.

The boys dismounted from their heaving horses.

"You had better sit down," suggested Lupe.

"Yes—" Mr. Ashley, wet and muddy, was trying to get his breath. "Thank you—my boy. You've saved—our lives! You—and your—companions—have done a brave thing. Your father will be proud of you, too—when I tell him." Gratefully, he looked up at Lupe. Then he looked anxiously at Charles and Ann who had sat down, exhausted, near him.

"We sure had a narrow escape," panted Charles. "Thanks, fellows. Thanks a million!"

"It is of no importance!" said the boys, altogether.

"That water, it fools people," said one boy named Tomás.

"We had no idea it was so—swift and treacherous," said Mr. Ashley. "When we found the car stuck—we tried to get out and walk. We had a late start from home, and we tried to cross this stream in a hurry."

"We will never forget your kindness," Ann told Lupe. She was shivering.

Lupe looked around for something to wrap about her, but his coat, too, was wet to the shoulders.

During the next few minutes, the running water sank

almost as rapidly as it had come rushing through the arroyo a short time before, like a tidal wave. Now it was only a foot deep around the wheels of the car.

"Tomorrow we'll come back with spades and dig it out," said Lupe. "You can lock it for the night, Mr. Ashley."

"Well, we won't sit here and freeze!" responded Charles wriggling all his muscles to keep warmer. As the sun set, a sudden chill was in the air, which made their wet clothes feel icy.

"You come now to the village for the procession," answered Lupe. "Father Ambrosius, he is waiting."

"But how will we get there?" exclaimed Ann.

"On horseback," Lupe explained, as he and Tomás mounted the horses again and urged the unwilling animals through the deep, sucking mud to the car. There the boys began to haul out coats and luggage.

Ann was still frowning in wonder as she threw about her shoulders the coat Lupe handed down to her.

"My friends here and I will ride two on a horse," said Lupe, when the car was emptied and locked. "Then, Mr. Ashley, you and your children can ride the other three horses." The boys began distributing the load to be carried.

"You boys are very kind. Thank you very much!" said Mr. Ashley, beginning to lead his horse with the others up the steep hill, before mounting.

The cavalcade rode slowly toward the sound of the distant Mission bell, which grew louder as the riders advanced.

Suddenly Ann exclaimed, "Doesn't it smell wonderfully of piñon and juniper? And something else," she sniffed.

"Maybe sage," suggested Lupe.

When they were well on their way, Ann and Charles chatted with Lupe and Tomás, riding double. There were only two more weeks before they would leave for the Pacific Coast, visiting the Carlsbad Caverns and the Grand Canyon on the way, they said. Then Ann would be going back to grammar school, but for Charles the new term meant his first year of high school.

"What about you, Lupe?" asked Charles.

"There is no high school at Las Trampas," replied Lupe quietly. "I finished grammar school in June. For me now I help on the ranch. I hope sometime I can go to school again."

"Oh, gosh!" sympathized Charles.

In the twilight and the silence, save for the pealing of the Mission bell, the dark, peaceful little village seemed like a dream place to the Ashley children, as they rode to Guadalupe's door.

Señora Romero was waiting to greet them. In her soft voice she bade them, *"Buenas noches. Pasen ustedes!"*

At once Lupe translated: "She says, 'Good-evening.

Will you pass in?' " He followed the visitors inside.

His mother smiled graciously, murmuring to each that the house was theirs! Then, by the light of an oil lamp, she and Lupe showed the visitors into their rooms. Ann saw first the little old wooden image of Saint Anthony in a niche in the plaster wall, before which a candle flickered in red glass. Charles, looking up at the long round beams in the ceiling, whispered, "Oh, boy!"

"Children," said Mr. Ashley, standing in the doorway of the large room which he and Charles were to share, "this looks like the room I slept in as a small boy at my great-grandmother's home. I feel like a child again. There was a blue-flowered pitcher and basin, with soap dish and toothbrush-holder to match, sitting on the brown marble top of a carved walnut washstand. A blue-and-white homemade rag rug! And the handsome high-backed beds and bureau to match the washstand!" He smiled at Señora Romero, as she set down the lamp on a marble-topped table.

The Señora, beaming with pleasure, nodded her head. "Long time 'go," she said in strange English, "Señor Romero's great-grandpapá he bring this furniture in ox-cart by Santa Fé Trail."

Now, while the Mission bell kept reminding them of their tardiness, the Ashleys hurried to change into clean clothes. Soon they were ready.

With effort Lupe opened the heavy handmade doors

of the church. His mother and guests entered with him into its cool fragrance of old fabrics, porous walls, and ancient woodwork, all saturated with incense. There was a rustling stir among those already gathered in the church. Only a few old women, kneeling on the clay floor praying, failed to lift their black shawl-covered heads.

Candles on the altar shed a luster over the dark surface of old paintings near them. In the candlelight the bunches of tissue-paper flowers in altar vases seemed real. The only lighting came from these candles and a few others in tin sconces on the walls.

Father Ambrosius entered, and vespers began. The Ashleys joined earnestly in the service there in the old Mission which for more than two hundred years had heard the prayers of the devout.

When the short service was over, the people moved toward the portal, where they all gathered. Then followed a bustle to light candles for the procession. The Ashleys had brought three dozen candles with them. Ann, her brother, and Lupe passed them to those near-by who did not have any.

Señora Romero, Mr. Ashley, and the three children took their places in the long double line that now began to form. The lighted candles lit up each serious face and showed the character of the brown hands holding the candles.

Now the sudden crackling of burning piñon wood could be heard. Tiny towers made of the wood had been placed ten feet apart in two rows. The towers had been built of sticks of piñon wood placed crisscross. The flames were leaping upward in each little tower as the sticks caught fire one by one. Charles looked questioningly at Lupe.

"They are *luminarias,*" he explained. "They light the path for the procession, around the plaza and around the Mission."

Presently the altar boys came with the golden cross and tall candlesticks to lead the procession. Behind them, four bareheaded men carried, on a small litter, an up-

right doll-sized image of Saint Bartholomew, the Patron Saint of the village. Long ago, when Las Trampas was first settled, the image had been carved of pine, and painted. Now it wore a lace-trimmed silk robe decorated with paper flowers. Father Ambrosius came next to lead the chanting of a short prayer in Spanish.

Over and over the chant was repeated as the procession slowly advanced. Black pitchy smoke with a spicy odor blew into their faces and swirled about them, as each person moved from the brightness of a tiny burning tower into shadow, again and again. In the cold breeze from the night-hidden mountains, candle flames streamed sideways, almost going out, and then sputtered

afresh to make shadows play over the faces of the people who bore the candles.

The front of the old church was lighted eerily by the little bonfires. The chanting in musical Spanish floated out into the crisp night air, accompanied by the ringing of the Mission bell.

"Oh, we'll never forget this—never!" Ann whispered to Señora Romero as they walked along, one behind the other. Guadalupe's mother smiled back at her.

As soon as the procession was over and people began to go home, Señor Romero came to greet his guests. After the ringing of the bell and the chanting, a peaceful silence spread over the Mission; and the canopy of bright stars seemed to come down close.

"I am glad to meet you," Señor Romero greeted Mr. Ashley. "Father Ambrosius say you are very good friends to our very old friends, the Browns, in Santa Fé."

Suddenly the Romero children appeared like ghosts out of the darkness.

"Father Ambrosius is *cawming!* He is *cawming* to our house!" said Marie excitedly, pulling on her mother's arm and speaking in English for the sake of their guests.

"Si (yes)," added little Rosa. "He is breaking the rule of no accepting the invitations to supper. He will eat at our house this one time."

"That is good," said Señora Romero. "Excuse, please," she said to Mr. Ashley, "we go queek home to get dinner." She and the little girls hurried away to their house, while the others waited to be joined by Father Ambrosius who was now wearing his usual black suit.

When they all reached the Romero home, they found a group of relatives and friends from out of the village, who had also been invited for the fiesta.

In the middle of the long, narrow living room, lighted by oil lamps, a long table had been set, with benches and odd chairs along its sides. The grown-ups sat at the table, Señor Romero at one end and Father Ambrosius at the other with Mr. Ashley at his right. Ann, Charles, Lupe, and his oldest sister, Sara, were also seated at the table.

Rosa, Marie, and four women relatives, all wearing gay-flowered cotton aprons, helped Señora Romero serve the food which they brought piping hot in big bowls from the kitchen stove. Little Agapito, with the other small children, sat at one end of the room awaiting quietly, but hungrily, their turn to eat.

The food was familiar to Lupe, but he was pleased when Ann and Charles exclaimed delightedly over its strangeness and said how good it tasted. He and Sara both replied quickly when Ann or Charles asked for the Spanish name for each dish. They also watched with amusement to see their guests taste the hot chili pepper sauce. Ann took the first mouthful. Swallowing quickly, she stuck out her tongue and began to pant. At the same time she reached hastily for her glass of water.

Sara caught her arm. "No," she warned. "Water makes the burning more hot. Eat some *pan,* some bread!"

Lupe had been busy naming the different foods, watching to see that Rosa and Marie did not spill hot coffee as they filled cups from gray enameled coffee pots, and telling about the quaint old pictures framed in tin on the wall. He had not been paying any attention to the talk of the grown-ups, until he suddenly heard his own name spoken. Then he began to listen.

"We're very proud of our Lupe," Father Ambrosius was saying. "He took highest honors when he finished our grammar school in June." Then the padre looked at Lupe with a kindly, teasing smile. "But he's a funny fellow. He thinks he can't live happily without seeing what the ocean is like and leaving the ranch to go away to school. No, Lupe?"

Lupe blushed and looked down at his plate. His father, with a twinkle in his eye, answered for him, "Yes, Lupe he has talked every day, since he was a leetle fellow, about seeing that ocean in his geography and about being a great lawyer. He likes it to help winnow the wheat and to ride the horseback, but I think those ocean waves they call to him all the time!"

Lupe's face grew pinker with the teasing. Then his breath almost stopped when Mr. Ashley spoke.

"This is good news for me, Lupe," he said, very seriously. "I have been wondering all evening how I could repay you in part for what you have done for me and my children today. Now I have a proposition to offer. Won't you go with us to see the Pacific Ocean? Then we would be so happy to take you home, as one of us, to go to high school with Charles in the fall. I'm sure he couldn't find a finer brother, which he has always wanted. And next summer we can all come back. Then Charles can get the taste of ranch life, which he has also longed for! How about it?"

Sudden silence had fallen upon the room. All eyes looked from Lupe to his father and mother, glancing at each other, and back to Mr. Ashley's earnest face.

"Oh, boy!" exploded Charles. "That'll be great!"

For a moment Lupe could not speak. In his mind he could hear the Mission bell ringing, for it was always during its gay pealing that he had dreamed of the blue oceans and built his aircastles of the future.

At last, *"Gracias!* Thank you, sir!" was all he could say. He looked from Mr. Ashley's kind face quickly to his father's.

"It is a good opportunity, my son. We thank Mr. Ashley very much!" agreed his father.

Then the boy looked at Father Ambrosius.

"Of course you must go," said the priest.

"It will make me very happy to go," said Lupe. *"Gracias!"*

Sudden happy chatter mingled with the scraping of chairs and benches as everyone stood up and crowded forward to congratulate Lupe. Everyone, that is, except the hungry younger children, who slid quickly into the emptied places at the table, intent only upon food.

Red River

ARIZONA

"PEACH SPRINGS! Peach Springs!" called the conductor as the *Grand Canyon Limited* pulled into the little station at Peach Springs, Arizona.

Harold and Roger Roberts, with duffel-bags slung over their shoulders, jumped off the train onto the station platform.

Tilting their wide-brimmed sombreros against the glare of the early morning sun, the two boys mingled with the crowd gathered on the platform of the little depot. There were townspeople who had come to see the arrival and departure of the train; cowboys in gay shirts and neckerchiefs, fringed chaps and jangling silver-trimmed spurs; and Hualapai (wal'la pye) Indians selling baskets of tanned rabbit skins, beadwork moccasins, and belts of horsehair.

"There he is!" exclaimed Roger.

"Hi!" called his brother, Harold.

Their Uncle Mason came toward them and greeted his nephews heartily. He led them over to his station wagon, loaded with camping equipment. Then, with the boys on the front seat beside him, he drove off, taking the road to the north.

They were soon out of the little town and had turned into the Hualapai Reservation, an almost uninhabited desert scarred by canyons and flanked by jagged mountains.

"This is like old times," Roger told his uncle as they jolted over the road. "Off on a Grand Canyon camping trip with you."

"Yes," added Harold. "But what about that special surprise you promised us?"

Their uncle replied good-naturedly, "Well, it wouldn't be much of a surprise if I told you ahead of time, would it?"

The boys laughed and agreed that he was right.

Uncle Mason was an engineer with the United States Bureau of Reclamation. He was starting out on his annual trip to inspect Boulder Dam and its great power plant. As had been his custom for several years, he had arranged this Easter vacation camping trip for his nephews.

The road followed a dry, shallow gully known as Peach Springs Draw. High above, three buzzards were flying around and around. The boys looked out across the desert, at the cactus plants and sagebrush, at the brilliant desert flowers—red Indian paintbrush and yellow poppies. On hillsides grew the yucca called "Spanish dagger" because the leaf resembled a blade. The Indians had named the plant "Candle of the Gods" be-

cause of its stalk of white flowers which grows ten feet tall. In the dry canyons stood the gnarled, black ironwoods, and where there was water, the cottonwood trees.

Near the head of the Draw, Uncle Mason stopped at a lonely, dome-shaped house where he said a friend of his lived. It was a hogan, or Hualapai Indian house, built of poles and branches, and covered with a thatch of juniper bark. Near-by were two corrals. Horses were in one of them. Uncle Mason explained the other corral was used to pen the flock of sheep, then grazing on the hills a half mile away.

As the boys and their uncle stepped out of the car, an old Indian appeared in the doorway of the hogan. He wore a buckskin shirt, blue overalls, and moccasins, and his hair fell in braids over his shoulders.

"Welcome again to my home, my friend!" he called.

"Chief Yaz-zih is kind to me and my nephews," replied Uncle Mason. Then he introduced the boys to the Indian.

The Chief led Uncle Mason and the boys into his hogan. Here, seated on the floor, they were invited to share a repast of quail and pancakes made of mesquite (mess keet′) meal.

When they had finished the repast, and were leaving, the old Chief walked out to the station wagon with his guests.

"May all your trails lead to the hogans of the gods,"

he said, giving them each a steady handclasp. "I hope you will come again."

After thanking him warmly for his hospitality, they were again on their way. Now the road wound steeply up hogbacks and over mesas. Finally, at the top of a long grade about thirty-five miles from Peach Springs, it came to a sudden end.

There, spread out before them, was the Grand Canyon of the Colorado! Lights and shadows played on the ranges of temple-like mountains that rose from the deep gorge. As the boys and their uncle watched, the mountains seemed to change color—crimson, lavender, purple, black; pink, yellow, saffron, brown. And down in the chasm, half a mile below, the red waters of the Colorado River followed its serpentine route as it had through countless ages.

The boys gazed spellbound into the Canyon. So intent were they that they did not notice the approach of a burro train until it came within a short distance of the car. Then, with a start, they looked around to see a line of seven burros with an Indian riding on the last one. Three burros had pack saddles and four had "westerns."

"The Indian is a Hualapai, employed by the Reclamation Service," said Uncle Mason. "He's come to take us down to the river."

"Is this the surprise?" asked Roger.

"Well—" began his uncle.

"It's a big enough surprise," declared Harold, "even if nothing else happens."

The Indian had ridden up to them now.

"Here's a couple of helpers for you, Tso," said Uncle Mason as he introduced his nephews. "Put 'em to work."

At once, the boys liked Tso. He was a tall man, dressed in cowboy's overalls and jumper, with sombrero and hiking boots.

While he packed the camping utensils and food on one of the burros, Roger and Harold packed the bedrolls and duffel-bags on two others. The boys shook out long ropes and secured the loads expertly. Then, mounting, the party left the station wagon and started down the steep Canyon trail, Tso leading.

The intense heat of the midday sun, reflected on bare rocks, soon made the riders remove their jackets and open their shirts at the necks.

For hours, the short, sharp drumming of the burros' hoofs against the rocks broke the silence as they followed the winding trail deeper into the Canyon.

By late afternoon, the trail had flattened out in the bottom of a sandy wash, and they heard in the distance the roaring of the river. Then, a mile farther on, the trail made a sharp bend onto a grassy flat of land flanked by a high cliff. There, a hundred feet below, rushed the red waters of the Colorado, tumbling, foaming, thundering in their course.

Wise to the trail and the ways of man, the burros stopped on the grassy flat.

"Pitch camp!" called Tso, above the roaring of the river.

Whistling, Roger and Harold took the saddles off the burros and put hobbles on their front legs to keep them from wandering. Tso laid out the four bedrolls on the ground near the base of the cliff and unpacked the food and cooking utensils. Uncle Mason brought armfuls of driftwood from where floods had cast it up along the river bank.

Carefully, Tso laid a fire in a small open grate made of stones piled one on another in a semi-circle. The stones were black with the smoke of many other campers' fires. Soon the acrid smoke rose from the pine slivers he used for kindling. Black smoke turned to gray as the hard woods took flame. Then there was the smell of broiling venison and dutch-oven bread as Uncle Mason and the boys prepared supper.

Afterwards, the four campers sprawled out on their bedrolls before a blazing log fire at the foot of the cliff.

"Long before the White Man ever saw the red river," Tso remarked quietly, "my ancestors camped here in the Canyon. Each night they gathered about a fire. It was the hour of contemplation when they prayed to their gods."

The thunder of the river seemed louder now in the

stillness of the settling night. Bats from caverns in the walls glided about the fire. Little gray night-hawks, like fleet shadows, darted at insects in the light of the blaze. Beyond the campfire loomed the darkness.

Then, above the sound of the river, came the howl of a coyote (kye′ote), shrill and dismal. It echoed away in the shadows of the Canyon. From a near-by tree, a western horned owl called "to-whoo-to-whoo!" The boys ducked under their blankets for the night.

The next morning, after breakfast, they packed the camping equipment on the burros and unhobbled them. Then Uncle Mason slung a rucksack over his shoulders. "D'you want to come along with me?" he asked the boys.

"Where are you going?" they wanted to know.

"Oh, that's part of the surprise. Tso's going back with the burros, and to get the station wagon. He'll meet us tomorrow."

"This sounds awfully mysterious," observed Roger, and his brother agreed.

Tso mounted his burro. *"Adiós* (good-by)," he said, waving his sombrero.

"Adiós!" called the boys as they followed their uncle.

It was a stiff hike downstream, over rough boulders and rocky banks, sometimes at the very edge of the swirling, tumbling river where the roaring of the water drowned out their voices. Then, leaving the river far below, they scrambled from rock to rock over great slides that all but dammed the gorge.

When they got back to the river's edge, the pounding of the rapids had dropped away. There, ahead of them, flowed the red waters of the river, wide and quiet.

"The headwaters of Lake Mead!" exclaimed Roger. "I know where we're going!"

"Sh-sh," warned Uncle Mason with a twinkle in his eye. "Maybe Harold doesn't know."

"Oh, I do!" Harold assured him. "And I think it's the best surprise in the world."

At the end of another mile, where a hogback jutted like a pointing finger into the widening lake, a fifty-foot cabin cruiser was waiting by a ledge.

"Hello, Mason!" called the man standing at the wheel. "You're right on time."

Uncle Mason introduced his nephews to Captain Foster, the pilot of the boat. Then another man appeared from the cabin and shook hands with the boys as they followed their uncle aboard. He was Jackson McHendry, a ranger in the National Park Service assigned to police the lake and its wild shores.

"You'll be on board for eight hours," the Captain told Roger and Harold, "so make yourselves comfortable."

"Thanks," said Roger. "After that hike through the Canyon, we'll be glad to take it easy."

"Off for Boulder Dam!" said Harold as they settled back in their chairs in the cockpit.

Soon the red waters of Lake Mead spread out wider. On either side rose the steep rocky shores. A flock of ducks took wing from ahead of the boat and disappeared in the gorge far upstream.

"The water's changing color," Roger suddenly announced.

The ranger explained that the sediment had begun to

settle when the river emptied into the lake. The heavier red silt had gone to the bottom, leaving the lighter, gray sediment. "In a few miles that, too, will disappear," he said, "and the lake will become deep blue and clear as crystal."

"We engineers call this 'stored water,'" said Uncle Mason, as he lighted his pipe and began to talk on his favorite subject. "You see, before Boulder Dam was built, the Colorado ran wild and uncontrolled. Every spring, when floods came, the river overflowed its banks, washed out dikes and railroads, and flooded rich farm areas. Then, later in the year, when water was most needed on the farm lands, all the floodwater had flowed away into the Gulf of California. It was wasted, you see, and there was seldom enough water left for irrigation purposes.

"Boulder Dam was built as a vast reservoir to hold back this water and release it when it is needed. Now there are no more devastating floods, followed by droughts. Thousands of desert acres have been reclaimed and turned into fertile farms for settlers.

"Boulder Dam even supplies cities on the Pacific Coast with water carried over desert and through mountains in a 250-mile-long aqueduct. Then, there's the electrical energy—but we'll talk about that another time. I see Jackson's getting lunch."

The hours went by quickly for the boys, looking out

over the clear blue lake with its steep jagged shoreline.

The boat passed Fortification Mountain, a great mass of red, blue, and yellow stone streaked with black. Then, just ahead, they saw the upstream face of Boulder Dam. Its white outline was reflected in the lake. The curving graceful arc of concrete reached up fully one hundred feet above the water and was anchored on both the Arizona and Nevada sides in the towering lava cliffs of Black Canyon.

They did not speak as they approached this mighty masterpiece of engineering. The boat glided past four circular towers, standing in the lake, two on either side. The boys knew that these were the intake towers through which water was released to the power plant and into the river at the downstream base below the dam.

A few minutes later, Roger and Harold stepped ashore while their uncle remained on board to check patrol records with the ranger.

They climbed up to a small platform carved out of the rock above the Arizona end of the dam. Leaning their elbows on the iron rail, they looked down.

There was the great concrete dam more than 700 feet high, acting as a "plug" across the Colorado where, through the ages, the river had slashed a narrow gorge between the two black mountains. Now, far below the crest of the dam, the released water roared and foamed into the river on its way through the deep, dark canyon to far-distant farm lands. At the base of the dam, the powerhouse looked as small as a paperweight. It stood with its back against the towering white wall of the dam.

"No wonder Uncle Mason is so proud of Boulder," said Harold quietly.

That night, the boys and their uncle slept in the guest room down in the powerhouse. When they crawled into their bunks, they felt very small and insignificant, listening to the roar of the water falling into the Canyon.

"Man-made thunder," was Uncle Mason's comment.

"So, this was the surprise," said Roger in a sleepy voice.

"It's the grandest surprise in the world," added Harold.

Their uncle laughed. "The *real* surprise is tomorrow morning."

Daylight came slowly in the depths of the Canyon, and Uncle Mason had been at work a long time when Tso arrived to call the boys for breakfast. Tso led them to the control room—a big central chamber where the walls were lined with complicated instrument boards from which the production and distribution of electrical energy were controlled. More than a score of men were already gathered there. "Governors of three states," Tso whispered, "officials and engineers of the Reclamation Bureau, and representatives of great power companies."

Uncle Mason left the group of men and crossed the room to meet his nephews. "I want you to be part of a very important ceremony," he told them. "This is really the surprise I promised you. When I give the signal, you are each to press one of these red buttons." He indicated two red disks on a panel of other red disks.

Then he turned to the guests. "We are here at Boulder Dam today," he said, "to put into operation two more generators in the battery of seventeen in this powerhouse. Like the others already in operation, they are among the largest in the world.

"Their combined electrical energy is widely distributed over our great Southwest. It is turning the wheels of cotton gins, factories, and mills in Arizona's Salt River Valley. It is lighting the deepest tunnels in Arizona's copper mines, and pumping water to transform arid desert acres into rich, verdant farms. It is grinding stone in a Nevada magnesium plant.

"Far to the west, in California, electrical energy from this plant is the very lifeblood of industry—the force that operates transportation lines and shipbuilding yards, fish canneries, textile mills, tire plants, and automobile and airplane factories."

Uncle Mason paused, glancing at his nephews who were standing ready by the panel of red disks.

"For untold centuries," he continued, "the red river raged through this canyon—the enemy of many, the friend of none. Today, it is 'harnessed'—the friend of man. Boys, you may push the buttons."

Promptly, Roger and Harold obeyed, their eyes shining with excitement at the importance of their roles in the ceremony.

The roar of water thundering into the Canyon gradually became louder. A sudden whine, high-pitched and shrill, hung in the air as new floods from the lake's intake towers poured into the giant new units. Then the roar and whine merged into the whirring music of turbines and generators.

Tso was the first to step forward and speak to the boys.

"The magic of the White Man has conquered the ancient canyon gods," he said quietly. "Now, from the might of the red river flows new strength for America."

GULF of MEXICO

MAINLAND of U·S·A

BAHAMA ISLANDS

AT

CUBA

HAITI

JAMAICA

CARIBBEAN SEA

CENTRAL AMERICA

PACIFIC OCEAN

Cristobal

PANAMA CANAL

SOUTH AMERICA

Here you may find the places where the children in the next three stories live.

These places are the Panama Canal Zone, Puerto Rico, and the Virgin Islands.

They are not a part of the mainland of the United States, as you can see. But they belong to the United States of America.

The Great Short Cut

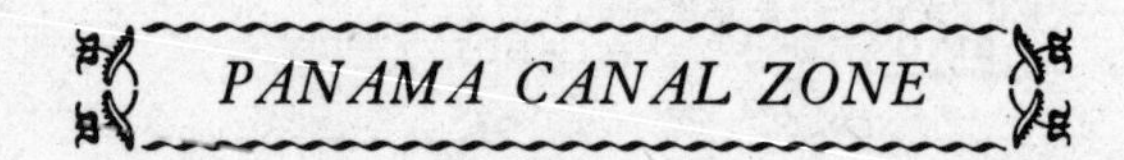

PANAMA CANAL ZONE

THE tropical morning sunlight glinted on the blue water of Limon (lee mohn') Bay. Mr. Barkely's small cabin cruiser rolled slowly with the rise and fall of the waves coming in from the Caribbean Sea.

The boat had left the dock at Cristobal (kris toh'b'l) just a few minutes before. Joe stood at the helm. He steered into the wide channel of the Panama Canal that ran through the Bay.

Joe was sixteen. He was a good navigator and weather prophet, and he often went into the Panama jungles as a guide. Mr. Barkely often hired him to come along on a week-end cruise.

Now, with his twelve-year-old son, Peter and Peter's friend, Tom Ainsworth, Mr. Barkely was taking his boat through the Gatun (gah toon′) Locks and on into Gatun Lake. He and the boys were going to spend a night at a camp in the jungle.

"This is keen!" exclaimed Tom. He stopped polishing a brass cleat and looked out over the channel. He had recently come from New Orleans to live in the Panama Canal Zone, and this was the first time he had been off with the Barkelys.

"Quite a parade of ships," said Peter, wringing out a mop with which he had been swobbing the deck. "There's a British freighter behind us in the channel, and the one ahead of us is flying the flag of the Republic of Panama. Perhaps they'll be with us going through the locks."

Mr. Barkely now came out of the cabin. "Here come two ships that've been through the Canal," he announced.

Tom and Peter stepped over to the port side. Quite near was a passenger ship flying the American flag. People were standing at the rail, and they waved to Mr. Barkely and the boys. Joe saluted with a single blast of the boat's whistle.

Mr. Barkely recognized the vessel as one which sailed on a regular route from South America. "They've come up the coast of Chile from Valparaiso (val pah rye′so)," he said, "and they're on their way to New York."

Now a small Dutch freighter passed the Barkelys' boat. The warm breeze carried a sweet smell from the lumber stacked on board. A sailor waved from the deck. Again Joe saluted.

"I guess the people on those ships are glad they didn't have to sail way around South America as vessels had to do before the Canal was opened," said Tom.

"Yes, it's a great short cut for interocean shipping," replied Peter's father. "The Canal saves 7,873 miles between San Francisco and New York."

"I should say the Canal *is* a short cut!" declared Tom.

On either side of the channel a tangle of tropical foliage could now be seen.

"Jungle," said Joe, grimly.

"Ever been in a jungle?" Peter asked his friend.

"No, I haven't," admitted Tom, "and I'd hate to go into one alone."

"So would I," said Peter. "The camp where we're going is in a dense jungle but, of course, Joe will be with us."

Tom and Peter stared into the depths of the dark green vegetation. It was like a wall shutting out the rest of the world. In among the foliage were giant-size ferns and festoons of long creepers. Here and there, the tangled mass of green was splashed with tropical flowers of brilliant colors.

Now and then a bird darted out of the leaves. Peter

pointed out to his friend a toucan (too kahn′), a black umbrella bird, cardinal canaries, and twittering green todies. Hummingbirds flashed in the sunlight like flying jewels.

"There's a troupial (troop′e al)!" Joe exclaimed, calling attention to a bird with markings of orange and royal blue. "Some folks call it a bugle bird," he added.

As the boat moved steadily along, Mr. Barkely and the boys heard the troupial's call—clear as a bugle.

Looking beyond the bow of the boat, Tom saw that they were now approaching the great Gatun Locks.

"Going through the Canal from the Atlantic, or Caribbean, end to the Pacific end," Mr. Barkely explained, "our boat will first be lifted from this sea-level waterway to the much higher level of Gatun Lake. Going the opposite way, boats are lowered to sea level."

On each side of a great concrete wall running parallel with the waterway, was an enormous steel gate.

"That Panamanian freighter is entering the lowest lock!" Peter exclaimed a few minutes later.

While his father steered their boat a short distance behind it, the freighter passed between the open sections of the great gate. Its engines had been stopped, and now, by means of hawsers attached to its bow and stern, it was being towed into the large concrete lock by four electric "mules," or locomotives. Two were running along a track on the high side wall of the lock. The other two were running on a track along the wide partition wall which separated this lock from the one on the other side for ships going in the opposite direction.

"Don't we get towed in?" Tom wanted to know.

"No, we don't," replied Peter. "Our boat is so small that Dad got permission to come into the locks under our own power."

Mr. Barkely was now steering through the great gateway and into the lock.

The side wall and the partition wall rose high above the cabin of the boat. The lock helper tossed a safety line to Peter who fastened it to the bow of the boat. Mr. Barkely shut off the engine, and the boat rocked gently.

A few minutes later the British freighter moved in through the gateway. The freighter's engines had been stopped, and it was being towed into the lock like the other freighter ahead.

"The gate's closing!" cried Tom excitedly.

He and the others watched while the steel sections gradually came together. Now the Barkelys' boat and the freighters were enclosed there in the lowest lock! It was like being in a huge swimming pool, Tom thought. As more water was let into the lock, the water level began to rise, and the boats rose with it.

"We'll be 'lifted' in each of the three locks as we go through. It's like going upstairs one step at a time," Joe explained to Peter's friend. "When we leave the highest lock, we'll be on a level with Gatun Lake—eighty-five feet above sea level."

While the water kept on rising, Joe explained further, "In the lock on the other side of the partition wall, the water is receding. The vessels in that lock have come through the Canal from the Pacific Ocean side. They are being lowered from the level of the Lake to sea level and will continue their voyage on into Limon Bay, the Caribbean Sea—"

"And the Atlantic Ocean!" Tom finished.

Now the water in the lock stopped rising. The gate at the farther end swung open. Being on a level with the water in the second, or next highest, lock, the Barkelys' boat and the freighters were now able to move into it. The freighters continued to be towed by the "mules."

As their boat was passing out of the third lock, Joe said, "Now we're on a level with Gatun Lake."

Soon Mr. Barkely had steered his boat out into the Lake.

"Let's find out where the freighters are going," said Peter. He called to a man in the stern of the Panamanian freighter, "Where are you bound for?"

"San Francisco!" came the reply.

Then from the stern of their own boat, Tom shouted to a seaman on the British ship behind them. "Where are you going?"

"Sydney, Australia!" came the reply.

Peter and his friend whistled.

Mr. Barkely then explained to Tom, "It'll take them about eight hours to make the entire trip through the Canal, which is about fifty miles long. After going through Gatun Lake, they'll pass through the Gaillard (gayl′erd) Cut which is on a level with this Lake. Then Pedro Miguel (pay′dro mee gel′) Lock will lower them to Miraflores (mee rah floh′rays) Lake. And the two locks on the other side of that Lake will lower them to the sea-level channel leading into Panama Bay on the Pacific side of the Canal."

Joe kept glancing up at the sky. A strong north wind

was blowing, and there were gray clouds above the northern shore of the Lake.

"I don't think Joe likes the look of the weather," Peter said to his friend. "He can usually tell when a tropical storm is coming. He's a good weather prophet."

"Son, suppose you take the helm?" Mr. Barkely suggested to Peter.

Peter took his place at the wheel while his father stood beside him. Tom looked out at the rolling hills surrounding the irregular shoreline of the Lake.

East of the locks, a train had left the Gatun Station for its run over to the Pacific side of the Isthmus of Panama. West of the locks, was the Gatun Dam with its great concrete spillway.

"Gatun Lake," Mr. Barkely told Tom, "is not a natural lake. It was made by damming up the water of the Chagres (char′gres) River across its valley there where it flows out to the Caribbean Sea. The Lake is a reservoir for the waters of the river and supplies water for the locks as well."

"The engineers who built those locks and thought up how to dam the river and make Gatun Lake and all the rest of this Canal must have been pretty smart," said Tom.

"They were," Mr. Barkely replied. "For centuries men had dreamed of cutting a canal across the Isthmus of Panama, or somewhere near it. All attempts failed, however, until the United States government finally succeeded in building this Canal which was opened to shipping in 1914."

A little later, Mr. Barkely took the wheel and made the turn in the channel for the long stretch of five miles to the cove on the Bohio (boh ee′ oh) Peninsula where he had planned to anchor for the night. The camp in the jungle was a half mile in from the shore. He was steering close to the edge of the channel.

When they were more than half way to Barro Colorado Island, Tom suddenly exclaimed, "Look at all those trees standing there under the water! That's a queer sight." He was staring down at the gaunt gray branches of innumerable trees the other side of the channel buoys.

"Once they were growing in the jungle," Peter told his friend. "Now, because the land is flooded over, they're standing under the Lake. It is a queer sight, all right."

Joe was looking at the sky again. "Mr. Barkely," he said in a quiet voice, "I think a 'norther' is coming."

"A norther!" exclaimed Peter's father.

"Yes, sir! I've been watching the sky since we left the locks. At first the clouds were blowing away. Now they've banked up thick, and they've turned black."

Mr. Barkely studied the sky to the north. "Shall we turn into one of the coves on Barro Colorado?" he asked Joe.

Joe studied the sky again before answering. "I think we should make a run for Bohio," was his decision.

By the time they were off Barro Colorado Island, the wind was whipping up the water of the channel. Spray was flying out from under the bow of the boat.

"I bet that tropical storm hits us hard before we get to Bohio," Tom exclaimed.

"I think we'll make it," Joe said.

Mr. Barkely steered past Bohio Point. Then he turned into the shelter of the cove.

"Well, we got here before the storm," said Tom. "You're a good weather prophet, Joe."

As soon as they had anchored near the shore of the jungle, Mr. Barkely remarked, "We'll start the galley stove and have something to eat."

After the meal, Mr. Barkely said, "Since that storm hasn't come yet, shall we start carrying some of our things in to camp?"

Peter and Tom looked at Joe who was frowning up at the sky. Some of the black clouds had broken away. The wind had died down a little. "Well—" he hesitated, "I figure we can just about make one trip up there."

"You and Tom can each carry one of the hammock rolls," Mr. Barkely told his son as he and Joe lowered the small native cayuca (kah yoo'kah), or dugout, which the boat carried. "I guess Joe can manage the other two. I'll stay here and get the rest of the things together."

Joe took the boys ashore in the cayuca. At first there seemed to be no place for them to land, but Joe's alert eyes soon found the opening he was seeking in the tangle of green foliage. He maneuvered the cayuca in and out among the snags and logs in the shallow water and got safely to the shore. An alligator slid into the water just ahead of the cayuca.

"Golly, I wouldn't want to step on him!" declared Tom while the others laughed.

Joe led the way up a sloping trail walled in with dense foliage of palm trees, tangled vines, and giant ferns. The leaves of the trees met overhead and an emerald-green light filtered through them.

"It's like walking in a green tunnel," observed Tom.

"I forgot my machete (mah chay'ta)!" exclaimed Joe suddenly. "I'll have to go back and get it. It won't take long. Don't move off this trail until I come back," he warned.

"We won't," Peter promised him.

Joe dropped the two hammock rolls on the ground by a palm tree, and retraced his steps.

"He never goes into the jungle without his big knife, or machete," explained Peter. "You never know when a machete will come in handy."

It was hot and breathless there in the jungle. The boys rested and then continued slowly up the trail.

Tom peered into the thick foliage on either side. A harsh-voiced macaw squawked from a tree, and the shriek of a parrot sounded through the jungle. Lizards rustled through the leaves on the path. A sloth hung from a branch just above the boys' heads.

Then both boys noticed that the wind had sprung up and that the emerald-green light was quickly fading. Rain began to splash on the leaves. The tropical storm had come!

"Joe was right," said Peter. "He told us we could just about make one trip to camp before the storm broke."

Now the treetops were tossing in the wind. The rain came down in torrents. It lashed through the thick foliage. Soon the boys were drenched.

"You'd think the spillway of Gatun Dam was over-head!" Tom shouted above the wind and the downpour of the rain.

It was almost dark now. Bowing their heads to the storm, the boys pushed on. Great ferns and fronds of palms were being blown about; some of them struck the boys' faces.

Suddenly, Tom shouted in a frantic voice, "Where's the trail?"

Peter was right behind him. Both boys stood still and tried to peer through the rain. All they could see was streaming water and the tangled foliage of the jungle. *They had lost the trail!*

"Don't take another step!" Peter ordered. "We can't find the trail in this storm, even though we can't be far from it. We'd better stand right here and wait for Joe to find us. He knows his way around in this jungle."

It seemed a long time before they heard Joe calling. They shouted in answer, and at last they could see him coming toward them. He was carrying the two hammock rolls over one shoulder. With his free hand, he was slash-ing at the leaves and low branches with his machete.

"It's a good thing you didn't try to keep on going," he shouted. "Come on—this way!" Cutting right and left with his heavy knife, he made a path through the jungle. A few yards farther on, they came to a small clearing. "Here's camp!" Joe grinned.

Almost as soon as they had dashed across to the wooden shed in a grove of banana plants, the rain had stopped. Soon the sun was out again. It shone here and there through the dripping wet vegetation.

Before going down the trail to get the rest of the camping things, Joe took a slingshot from a nail in the shed. "We'll give Mr. Barkely a surprise for supper," he said.

While Peter and his friend watched, Joe picked up a stone and held it in the sling. His alert eyes followed around the edge of the clearing. He took aim. The boys held their breath.

"Good shot!" said Peter a moment later.

Joe ran over to a banana plant and picked up a small rabbit. "This is a *conejo pintado* (kon ay'ho peen tah' do)," he told Tom. "That means a painted rabbit. It will make a good *sancocho* (sahn koh'cho)—stew—for supper."

Hundreds of parakeets were screeching from the trees as Tom and Peter, with Joe leading, started back through the jungle trail.

Adiós, Villa del Río

PUERTO RICO

ALL was quiet at Villa del Río at eight o'clock that Monday morning. It was January second. After the bustle of early chores, the large frame house on the Puerto Rican farm hardly showed signs of life except for a few chickens pecking in the garden.

Presently, up the path from the stable came Pedro (pay'dro), the handyman, leading a beautiful white saddle horse. He crossed the back yard and tied the animal to the iron ring in the trunk of the almond tree behind the house.

"Doña (dohn'ya) María," he said, coming to the back door. "Please give me the side-saddle now. Your orders were that I should start for town at eight o'clock to get Niña Carmencita (neen'ya kar men see'ta)."

"Yes, Pedro." Doña María spoke from the kitchen. Then she said to Juanita (whahn nee'ta), the cook, "Bring the side-saddle from the closet. Carmencita telephoned from town last evening that she's coming to visit for a few days and wants to use the saddle today. It's a sudden whim *la nena* (nay'na) seems to have."

Doña María often called her niece *la nena,* meaning

"the little girl," as they had done when she had lived on the farm as a small child. Her niece called Doña María "Tía (tee'a) María," which is Spanish for "Aunt Maria." Pedro called Carmencita "Niña Carmencita" which is Spanish for "Miss Carmencita," or simply *niña* meaning "Miss." Now Carmencita was twelve and lived in town with her parents.

Pedro went back to where the horse was standing and kept brushing the already shiny coat until Juanita came out.

"I don't see why Niña Carmencita wants to ride to-day," he told the cook when she had brought the saddle in a heavy cloth bag. "And of all things, she wants the side-saddle! For a long time now, she has come out to the farm in the car, or by bus. But today she wants to ride."

"It's a whim she has," said Juanita, repeating what Doña María had just told her.

Pedro helped Juanita pull the fine saddle out of the bag. "This isn't Niña Carmencita's saddle at all, you know," he said. "It belongs to her mother. *La niña* rides astride, as all girls do now, but she has taken a sudden fancy to the side-saddle."

Soon he had saddled the white horse. Then, riding another horse, Pedro started for town, leading the white horse by the bridle.

"It will be nice to see *la nena* again," declared Doña María after he had disappeared down the road. "She's so busy these days in town with her school and her friends that she doesn't come out to see me as often as she used to do."

"But why does she want to ride the white horse?" asked Juanita.

"She doesn't want to come by bus any more, and she doesn't want her parents to drive her out. It's a—a whim, as I've already told you." Doña María tried to sound light-hearted, but she frowned. She knew it was more than a whim that made her niece want to ride the white horse out to the farm.

For some time Carmencita had been ready, waiting

on the balcony of the house in town where she lived with her parents—Doña Carmen and Don Enrique (dohn ahn reek'). Then she saw Pedro riding into the street, leading the white horse by the bridle. Now she could hear the *clop-clop* of the horses' hoofs as he rode up to the house with its white walls and black grille gate.

"There's Pedro!" she called to her mother. Then she ran inside. "Do help me with the skirt," she said.

Doña Carmen smiled. "Not only do you insist upon using my side-saddle," she told her daughter as she fastened the light-green skirt over her dress, "but you borrow my riding-habit as well. Here, let me help you into the jacket. Now, you do look grown-up!"

Carmencita tried to smile. "All of a sudden—I don't feel grown-up at all—" Her lip was quivering.

"Now, now," said her mother. "You told us last evening that you wanted to look grown-up from now on when you went out to the Villa del Río."

"I know I did," replied Carmencita, "and I hope Tía María and the others will think I look grown-up. But I—I guess I'm still *la nena,* after all."

"You had better start right along," was her mother's suggestion. "Your father and I will drive out this evening to spend a day or two with you and Tía María."

Carmencita lifted her head proudly, and her voice didn't waver as she said, "Yes, Mother."

A few moments later she came out through the gate.

"How grown-up you look, *niña,*" Pedro greeted her.

Soon the *clop-clop* of the horses' hoofs sounded on the highway that led from town to the open country.

"Every week-end, and every holiday from now on, Pedro," said Carmencita, "I wish to ride the white horse to the farm. But why I wish to do it—that is a secret, Pedro."

"Yes, *niña,*" said Pedro.

Silently they rode toward the farm. The tropical sun was warm, though the hour was only ten. It shone through the flaming red blossoms of the trees on either side of the road, making them look as though they were on fire. Farther along the road were rows of orange trees with their deep yellow fruit hanging from the branches. There were palm trees, too, with their shaggy green tops shining in the sunlight.

Now, Carmencita and Pedro were leaving the highway for the dirt road that led into the broad, fertile valley where Don Enrique's fields of sugar cane were.

Carmencita remembered how last October when she had come out to the farm for the long week-end of Columbus Day, she had seen the blossoming cane. Its grayish-white plumes moving gracefully in the breeze had made her imagine an army of knights wearing plumed helmets. Now there were no blossoms, but the tall cane was moving in the breeze and the fields looked like a light-green ocean.

"Have they started cutting the cane?" Carmencita asked as she gazed ahead at the fields.

"Yes," replied Pedro. "The field by the river is being cut. They started last week, and, my! the stalks are as thick as my wrist. Don Enrique has an especially good crop this year."

As they came out of a dip in the road, and Carmencita could see the farmhouse ahead, she straightened her shoulders. "This is how I must remember it," she said to herself. "The dear old white-painted house in the grove of almond trees." Then she saw her aunt and the cook at the side door, waving to her. "And I shall remember Tía María and Juanita waiting to welcome

me. That is how I shall think of the Villa del Río—always."

A few minutes later, at the side door, Pedro helped her from the saddle. Doña María smiled broadly and embraced her. "How grown-up you look!" she exclaimed, and Juanita said the same thing. "Come right in, *nena,* and get out of those grown-up clothes this very minute, and start having a good time."

"Oh, I want to do all the things I always loved doing here," declared Carmencita.

"Pilar (pee′lar) is coming over directly after lunch," said Juanita.

Carmencita smiled. She and Pilar were old friends. Pilar was the daughter of the tenant farmer who lived across the field near the brook.

"Well, this is like old times," declared Doña María as she greeted Pilar after lunch. "Now, run along and have a good time."

The children ran out-doors. They were wearing bandannas over their hair because of the heat of the sun.

"I want to do everything—everything we always used to do," said Carmencita as she led the way along the path that led to the brook.

"But why?" asked Pilar. "You haven't come out to visit your aunt since last fall. And now you suddenly want to do everything we used to do."

"It is a secret," replied Carmencita. "I'm not to tell anybody until the right moment."

"Will you tell me, first of all?" asked Pilar.

Carmencita promised, "Yes, Pilar. You, first of all."

The girls stopped by the giant rose apple tree growing at an angle from the low bank of the brook.

"Let's climb out on the big limb," suggested Carmencita, "as we always used to do."

The girls climbed into the tree and then sat out on the low branch which swayed up and down just above the brook. Now, they heard a familiar sound. It was accompanied by a *tap-tap-tap* and the gurgle of water.

"That's your mother singing, Pilar!" exclaimed Carmencita. They leaned far out on the branch and looked up the brook. There, beyond the branches of other trees on the bank was Pilar's mother doing her laundry. "Let's go and say 'hello'!"

"See who is here!" Pilar's mother said joyfully as the girls came along a few minutes later. "I saw you riding past on the white horse this morning," she added as she rubbed her laundry up and down on a large stone. "You looked very grown-up."

"Please!" said Carmencita. "I'm just a little *jibarita*."

Pilar's mother nodded. A *jibarita* meant a country person. "True, you were born at the Villa del Río," she said, "and I know you love the old place, but now you are really a young lady from town."

"No!" exclaimed Carmencita. "I'm only twelve—I'm not really grown-up. But from now on, I want to *look* grown-up when I come riding out to the farm. If I look grown-up, maybe I'll act grown-up—" She paused and then went on, "and not show how sad I feel when I see the old house and Tía María and Juanita waiting for me."

Pilar and her mother glanced at each other, but they remained silent and did not ask any questions.

After playing along the brook for a while, Carmencita suggested to Pilar, "Let's go and find Pedro and ask him to take us to the field by the river where the cane is being cut."

"Yes," agreed her friend, "as we always used to do."

They found Pedro in the stable, mending a piece of harness. Soon he was leading the way to the cane field.

As they walked along, Carmencita asked Pilar, "I always like to watch the men swinging their machetes (mah chay'tayz), don't you?"

"Yes, but remember the fuzz," Pilar reminded her. "We mustn't get too near, or the fuzz will make us itch."

Carmencita laughed. "Oh, Pilar, I wouldn't mind that. I don't want to miss *anything* from now on at the farm. The next few months will be my last chance to do everything I love to do before I—"

Pilar exclaimed, "Your last chance! Why, what do you mean?"

Carmencita bit her lip. "Nothing," she replied. "Make believe I didn't say it, Pilar." She turned her head so that her friend wouldn't see the tears in her eyes.

Pilar stared at her in astonishment, but she remained silent as they walked along after Pedro.

Now, in the distance, they could see the men working, harvesting the cane. The graceful, light-green stalks were over ten feet tall, and their leafy tops were moving in the breeze.

As they approached, they saw a familiar figure. It was Pilar's father, Modesto. With machete in hand, he was helping the workers to cut down the cane to the level of the ground. The children and Pedro watched while they hacked off the leafy tops. There were great piles of stalks heaped on the ground, waiting to be loaded onto oxcarts.

Now came the sound of the creaking of a cart moving along the narrow, rutted road that went winding across to the side track on the other side of the field. From there, the track led to the main line which went on to the large sugar refinery.

Slowly, the lumbering, reddish-brown oxen drew the cart, while the man driving them called out, "Oo-ee-say! —Hey!—Oo-ee-say!" Then he burst into song,

> "Ay! Le, le, le, le, le, le!
> The stars in the skies
> Are a hundred and four,

But your beautiful eyes
Make two starlets more!"

The driver's voice wavered on the long notes because of the bumping of the cart over the ruts in the road. Now he drove up to one of the piles of stalks, and the oxen stopped and stood patiently as he jumped to the ground.

"I'll get you girls some sugar cane," offered Pedro as he walked over to the workers.

"I'm so glad he remembered," Carmencita told Pilar.

Pilar laughed. "I was going to run over and get a piece myself," she admitted, "but I didn't want to have any of that fuzz on me."

Pedro returned with a nice green stalk of cane. He whipped his knife out of his pocket and skinned the stalk. Then he carefully cut off the joints and split each of the sections into four pieces. These he gave to Carmencita and Pilar.

The girls chewed the sugar cane and watched as other oxcarts drove up and the workers piled them high with the long stalks. Each load was bound with chains lying in the bottom of the cart. Then the load could be lifted easily by a crane from the cart into one of the cars waiting on the side track. Now the loaded carts moved off on the road that led to the side track.

"Well, that's the last of the cane to be cut today," remarked Pedro.

"Let's go over and see the engine take the cars away," Pilar suggested.

Still chewing on the sugar cane, they hurried after the last oxcart. Pedro had a hard time keeping up with them.

Seven cars were lined up on the track, and the crane lifted the loads from the carts and placed them in the last car to be loaded. Now a little steam engine came puffing and panting from the main track. It left a string of empty cars for the next day's cutting. Then it was ready to pull the loaded ones out of the siding.

"Come, back, back! There, hold!" called a man who was attaching the cars. Then he shouted, "Go ahead!"

The engine pulled the seven cars loaded with Don Enrique's sugar cane out of the siding and on to the main track. Then it speeded away down the valley, on toward the sugar refinery, whistling loudly to warn the next farm of its coming.

Carmencita sighed as she turned away and walked back to the farmhouse with Pilar and Pedro.

On Thursday, Carmencita's visit was over. Friday was January Sixth, Three Kings Day. She had always been home for that special day, celebrated in Puerto Rico. According to the old Spanish custom, Three Kings Day commemorated the visit of the Three Kings to the manger in Bethlehem. It was the day when children expected the Three Kings to leave them presents, just as children in other places expected Santa Claus to leave gifts on Christmas Eve. This year, Carmencita hoped the Kings would leave her a wrist-watch—her first one!

Out in front of the house, Doña María, Juanita, Pilar, and Pedro were waiting for Carmencita to leave. It was almost time for the bus. There it was now, turning the bend in the road.

"Come again soon, *nena,*" urged Doña María. "And here is the riding-habit for you to wear the next time." She gave her niece a neatly-wrapped bundle. Then she said, *"Adiós* (ah dee os')," which, in Spanish, means "good-by."

"You look so grown-up when you wear the riding-habit," Juanita reminded her.

"Yes, I—" Carmencita hesitated. Then as the bus stopped beside her, she added, "I have to look grown-up now whenever I come."

They all stood waving, and Pilar kept on waving until the bus disappeared in the dip of the road. She was thinking over what Carmencita had told her—that the next few months would be her last chance to do everything that she loved to do there on the farm. What did she mean by that, Pilar wondered.

Nearly every week-end now, Carmencita came out to the farm. Pedro rode into town, leading the white horse with the side-saddle, and Carmencita rode back, always wearing the riding-habit that made her look so grown-up.

With spring came the planting of new sugar cane. Then the summer came with its long days. Now the flamboyant trees were brilliant with flaming blossoms. On the farm, the guava trees were heavy with fruit.

Then came a week-end early in the fall. Carmencita and Pilar had walked down to the brook and were now sitting out on the limb of the giant rose apple tree. Below them the water was dappled with sunlight. Near-by, Pilar's mother was singing as she did her laundry.

"Now, Pilar," began Carmencita, "I will tell you why I have been coming out to the farm so often, and why I've been doing everything I love to do here."

"Ever since the winter, I have been wondering," admitted her friend.

"Pilar—" Carmencita felt the tears coming into her eyes. "I'm going away tomorrow!"

Pilar gasped. "Going away?"

"Yes, I'm going to boarding school in the States," said Carmencita. "It's the same school where my mother used to go. I shall come back every winter vacation, and for the lovely, long summer vacations—always. Oh, I shall miss things here. That is why I've been doing everything that you and I have always loved doing, over and over again." Carmencita had succeeded in blinking back her tears. "We must write to each other every week."

Pilar nodded and said sadly, "Every week."

"Here," said Carmencita, "this is for you, Pilar."

Through her own tears, Pilar saw her friend fasten something on her wrist. She blinked hard. It was a charm bracelet that Carmencita had received on last Three Kings Day, when she had received her first wrist-watch.

"For me, Carmencita?" Pilar managed to ask. "For me?"

The next day, everybody at the farm was standing out in front of the house. Don Enrique had telephoned from town to let Doña María know when the plane would be passing overhead. Now the droning of the motors suddenly filled the air, and the plane appeared, flying low. The sunlight shone upon it. They all waved and called softly *"Adiós"*—good-by.

"I shall miss her very much," said Doña María.

Pilar waved until the plane carrying Carmencita away from them was only a speck in the sky.

For many a day after that, Pilar, Pedro, Juanita, and Doña María all stopped whatever they were doing when they heard over the farm the drone of airplanes headed north. Above the roar of the motors they seemed to hear a familiar voice say, *"Adiós, Villa del Río."* And they missed Carmencita all the more.

The Masquerade

VIRGIN ISLANDS

A WARM breeze from the Caribbean Sea was blowing into the harbor of St. Thomas, one of the Virgin Islands. It stirred through the streets and gardens of Charlotte Amalie, the only town on the island.

As Clayton Baxter walked along one of the streets, he heard the distant rattle of derricks at the waterfront. He knew that the harbor was one of the most important in the West Indies, for it was a port of call for ships bound for the Panama Canal, as well as for ships coming from the Canal on their way to Europe. Often, after school, he liked to go down to the piers to watch the loading and unloading of the ships, and to see the passengers going aboard or disembarking. This afternoon, however, he had something else to do.

Clayton was on his way to see his school friends, Oliver and Oclevia Jackson. He had found a note from them on his desk when he had come in from baseball practice. "Please see us about something urgent," was their message. What could this be, he wondered.

He turned into a narrow street on the outskirts of town where the small houses were painted white, gray, orange, yellow, or blue. Some were built out to the sidewalk and had overhanging balconies from their second floors. Others were set back from the street behind fences or garden walls.

"Hello, Clay!" Oliver was calling to him from the balcony of his house across the street. His sister, Oclevia, was there with him. She had blue bows tied on her black pigtails.

Clayton waited for a horse-drawn cart to pass. It was heaped with large bunches of bananas and was driven by a man in a wide-brimmed straw hat. Then the boy crossed the street to his friends' house.

Soon the three children were sitting out on the balcony eating pieces of sweet coconut sugar cake which Mrs. Jackson had made for them.

"We want to talk to you about Aunt Clarissa—," began Oclevia.

"Aunt Clarissa?" questioned Clayton. Everybody in the neighborhood knew old Aunt Clarissa and liked her because she was always so good to people. "What's happened?"

Oclevia told him, "She fell in her vegetable garden this morning and hurt her ankle. The doctor says she mustn't leave the house."

"Not even to go to the market," added Oliver.

Old Aunt Clarissa made her living by taking her farm

products to market. Each morning, early, she walked to the market place from her little house outside of town. On her head she balanced a wooden tray. It was filled with vegetables or mangoes or bunches of sweet little finger bananas. She remained at the market most all day, and when she returned home, she carried the empty tray on her head.

"How'd you find out about her accident?" Clayton was curious to learn.

"Mother found out," replied Oclevia. "When Aunt Clarissa didn't go by to market as usual this morning, Mother went to her house to see what was the trouble. The doctor was there putting a bandage on her ankle. He's coming tomorrow, too, to see if the swelling's gone down. He's given her some medicine, and she must stay home two weeks."

Clayton whistled. "Two weeks! How's she going to sell her vegetables and things?"

"Mother's going to sell them for her at the market," explained Oliver. "But come on, we'll talk about it at Aunt Clarissa's. We're going there now."

High above their heads, the breeze rustled the shaggy tops of the tall palm trees as Clayton and the Jackson children walked toward Aunt Clarissa's little two-room house on the farm.

They found her sitting by the window in her front room which was cluttered with furniture and papered with pages cut from mail-order catalogs. She was resting her foot on a cushion and reading a mail-order catalog. She smiled at her visitors when they opened the screen door and entered the room.

The children sat down in rocking chairs and began to rock back and forth. They glanced curiously at a little table near the door upon which was set an array of glassware. They also looked at the small round table in the center of the room, where Aunt Clarissa always kept a queer assortment of things. There were wax flowers in a vase, three pincushions, a conch shell, and framed photographs of her two nieces. Clayton and his friends knew that her nieces also lived in the Virgin Islands; one

lived on the island of St. John, and the other on the island of St. Croix.

Aunt Clarissa now began to talk in her slow drawl. "I have to stay home for two weeks. Mrs. Jackson says she'll sell my vegetables for me, but what worries me is who's going to pick them and carry them to the market."

Oclevia spoke up with enthusiasm, "That's what we came to talk about. Oliver and I are coming early every morning, before school—"

"So am I," interrupted Clayton, deciding at once that he was to be included in the plans, whatever they were.

"—and pick things for you," Oclevia continued. "We'll carry them to the market."

Old Aunt Clarissa smiled. "That's very good of you."

"You're always doing kind things for other people," Clayton reminded her.

"Now's our chance to do something kind for you," concluded Oclevia.

"Thank you," said Aunt Clarissa. "And now, Oclevia, you may please fix my supper for me. The fish is already to fry, and the fungi (fun′jye) is ready to heat up."

Oclevia started to fry the fish in a charcoal pot behind a screen, and to stir the corn meal which Aunt Clarissa called "fungi." Then Aunt Clarissa closed the mail-order catalog and sighed, "What with paying the doctor and buying medicine, I won't be able to buy anything out of this catalog for a long while."

During the following week, Clayton and his two friends got up early every morning and walked out to Aunt Clarissa's. They picked vegetables, mangoes, and little bananas, and carried them to the market where Mrs. Jackson was waiting to sell them. Then the children went on to school.

One morning when they were on their way to school from the market, they met the doctor. He thanked them for helping Aunt Clarissa, and added, "I'm going to drive her to the market next Saturday. A cruise ship is coming in from New York and there'll be a lot of people around. She'll be able to sell them her little finger bananas."

"Cruise ship!" exclaimed Clayton as he and his friends continued their way. "Let's ask some of the boys and girls to help us get up a masquerade at the market. We'll collect money and give it to Aunt Clarissa. Then she'll be able to buy something else from the mail-order catalog!"

"That's what we'll do," said Oliver, and Oclevia added, "And it'll be a lot of fun. But, of course, we won't tell Aunt Clarissa. We'll give her a big surprise."

Clayton suggested, "We'll fix some dried 'squashes,' too, and—" But before he could say anything more about these native musical instruments, they were at school.

The next Saturday afternoon, a good many passengers from the cruise ship had left their hotels and were sitting on benches in the park. The green of the mahogany trees and the palms shut out the sun's glare and cast dark shadows on the paths which were bordered with red hibiscus (hye bis'kus).

During the day, the visitors had been strolling about the quaint city of Charlotte Amalie. They had gone into the shops to buy American or British goods, French perfumes, or Danish silverware. They had visited the "Co-op," or store, where native handicraft was on sale. There they could buy hand-embroidered linens, woven palm mats, baskets, hats, or tortoise-shell jewelry. Some of the cruise passengers had also bought things which were on display at the curbs along the streets, under the palm trees.

Now, they seemed content to be sitting there in the park, resting. At first they did not notice the small group of boys quietly gathering around one of the benches.

Then, suddenly, they began to hear queer sounds as the children started to play on their dried "squashes." They had made these instruments by filing lines across the squashes, over which they were now scraping pieces of wire. *Which-ero—which-ero—which-ero!* came the sounds, over and over again.

One of the boys now jumped up on the bench and announced, "Come to the masquerade at the market!"

Which-ero—which-ero—which-ero!

Laughing and talking, most of the people followed

the boys to the market where they strolled about admiring the things on display.

It was a gay scene. There were natives standing beside patient little donkeys loaded with oranges. Other venders had their wares in crates or in trays or baskets. There were vegetables, fish, and many kinds of fruits, such as mangoes, sea grapes, papayas (pah pah'yahz), pineapples, melons, limes, and bananas.

Some of the venders were dressed in white clothes and wore large brimmed hats or kerchiefs. Other people were wearing brilliantly colored dresses of gay flower designs, and high-crowned straw hats. These people were of French descent. Their ancestors had come to the West Indies from Normandy and Brittany as long ago as the seventeenth century.

The boys had now stopped playing on their "squashes." They had taken their places near one special vender. She was an old woman with a plaid kerchief on her head. Her kind black face was wrinkled into a smile.

"Finger bananas!" old Aunt Clarissa called in her slow drawl as the visitors came gathering around her. Soon all of the sweet little bananas had been sold, and she dropped her money into her pocket.

"Where's the masquerade?" asked one of the visitors.

Again the boys played on their "squashes." This seemed to be a signal. The next moment everybody was clapping as Clayton came walking on stilts from the

other side of the market. He was dressed in a pink dress and wore a wig made of rope. Clayton was followed by a boy who was dressed in a clown's costume, half red and half white. He had a large false head with a smiling mouth and enormous bulgy eyes. Clayton leaned over and took the clown by the hand, and the two boys did a slow dance.

"Good! Good!" Everybody laughed and applauded.

Now other children appeared from the other side of the market. Some of the girls were dressed in their mothers' old clothes and hats, while some of the boys were "pirates" with black patches over their eyes. Two girls, in gypsy costumes, entertained the audience by dancing the bamboula while a boy beat upon a drum. When the dance was finished and the clapping had stopped, all the children stepped aside to make way for a "bear" and its trainer.

The "bear" was Oliver dressed in two burlap bags. The upper one had holes for his eyes and slits cut out for his arms. His feet stuck through the bottom of the other bag, and the costume had been sewed together at his waist. Oclevia was the trainer. She was wearing a red cotton dress and red ribbons on her black pigtails. She led her brother by a rope tied under his arms.

"Ladies and gentlemen—" Clayton began while everybody looked up at him on his stilts. "Oclevia Jackson will now show off her trained bear!"

Now the audience applauded and then watched closely as Oclevia gave a yank on the "bear's" rope and called out, "Dance, bear! Dance!"

Oliver danced and performed other antics. He stood on his head. He walked upside down on his hands. He turned somersaults. He danced again. Then he rolled over and over, and stopped right in front of old Aunt Clarissa who clapped her hands and said in her slow drawl, "Good! Good!"

Now Clayton got down from his stilts and picked up Aunt Clarissa's wooden tray and passed it around the audience while the people clapped and cheered Oclevia and the "bear." When Clayton brought the tray back to Aunt Clarissa, it was filled with coins!

"Thank you for coming to the masquerade!" Clayton called out as the people walked away, again laughing and chatting.

Which-ero—which-ero—which-ero! Scraping on their "squashes," the boys moved off down the street, followed by the masqueraders.

Now Clayton and the Jacksons were the only ones left there with Aunt Clarissa. Oclevia was helping Oliver out of his costume.

Old Aunt Clarissa was staring down at the coins in her tray. "I do thank you," she told the children. "Now I can get another rocking chair from the mail-order catalog." Her kind old face was wrinkled into a smile.